Praise for the Book

It was a great pleasure reading your short stories, a field you have mastered very well. In my personal capacity I can say that they are engaging beyond words!

The empowerment of female characters in your stories is admirable. In today's time, as we focus on girls becoming strong women, it is heartening to see how beautifully you have portrayed their resolves. You are a master of flawless, short and emotionally powerful expression. Your stories remind us that somewhere and sometime in our past we have lived through your characters. It is like rewinding our own life movies.

More power to your pen, Sumita!

—**Alka Raza,** Chairperson of the Centre for Gender Equality and Inclusive Leadership (CGEIL) at XLRI—Xavier School of Management, Jamshedpur

A fascinating collection of short stories, each having something that has a direct relation with the author. 'Banyan Tree', elegantly written and surely Sumita's favourite genre, keeps the reader on edge with its build up into a supernatural thriller!

'Gram Dida', 'The Confetti' and 'Playhouse Park Street' are three women-centric stories, a bold feature of Sumita's earlier writings. The women, including the 'Gram Dida', are strong, living life on their own terms and taking life changing decisions, not averse to keeping their lips sealed about something dark in the past, if it helps in making the future bright!

I can see so much of the author in both, 'The Deal' and 'Close Encounters'. An engrossing story of a young school student and his parents, all in need of moral lessons, 'The Deal' also showcases Sumita's professional background as an Educator and Counsellor. 'Close Encounters' is a beautiful collection of many stories within one story. Personally, I am particularly inspired by this story, tempted to go back in my past and search for stories forgotten.

—**Raj Kanojia,** Information Commissioner, West Bengal, and former Director General of Police

In Banerjea's carefully crafted short stories, characters grapple with everyday realities that emerge out of their social situations and individual actions. They realize themselves and their potentials during moments of conversation, confession, self-analysis, and artistic expression. And in the process they form meaningful and transformative relationships with other humans and non-humans. Set amidst urban and rural environments, each scenario invites us to sensitively face our truths and reach out across differences and divides to enable mutual learning and growth.

—**Vishal Khandelwal**, Historian of Art and Architecture, Harvard University, USA

PLAYHOUSE PARK STREET

SUMITA BANERJEA

Readomania

Readomania
An imprint of Kurious Kind Media Private Limited
readomania.com
contact@readomania.com | Facebook: @iamreadomania |
X: @iamreadomania | Instagram: @iamreadomania

First Published in 2023 by Readomania. Reprinted in 2025.

Edited by Indrani Ganguly

ISBN: 978-93-91800-43-7

Typeset in Palatino Linotype by Shine Graphics
Printed in Delhi

Dedicated to

My Parents...

Contents

Foreword

Empathic listening is the key to figuring out what people are really about.

Sumita Banerjea has done a lot of this in her life, because she is fascinated by *why* people do what they do.

And she presents a delightful rainbow of reasons through this collection of stories.

Four—sometimes overlapping—themes cut across most of her stories:

First, what sparks human agency? What makes someone say enough is enough? In 'Mrs. Sharma', the protagonist reaches a tipping point of tolerating her husband's condescension, and decides to carve her own path. As does Inder's mother in 'The Deal'. 'Gramdida' faced with rape, "did the only thing she could"—she bit her offending brother-in-law's hand. It was a matter of saving herself, it wasn't about cool decision-making. Each story presents a new colour of a trigger for agency.

Second, which of the multiple identities that we all juggle rises to the top when agency is sparked? In 'Legacy', Aarnavi puts her inner tigress to work when that was the only way to safeguard her legacy for her children. In the story 'Playhouse Park Street', Avasa finds peace in finally residing comfortably in her true identity, when the secret of her parentage surfaces.

Third, discovering your core identity, that subsumes all the others when push comes to shove, is basically discovering the truth about yourself. What are the avenues to this profound truth? And what on earth do you do with it? Sometimes, you martyr yourself to a truth that society foists on you, but extend the benefit of the discovery to the next generation, as Roddur Sen did in 'Invincible'. Or, obvious truth simply presents itself through the mouth of babes, as it does in 'Angel's Trumpet'. Sometimes, the truth-seeking journey is painful, as it was for Nathan in 'No Less A Son', in which he finally finds peace in his mother's and his own acceptance of his sexual orientation, despite his father's rage.

The last major theme reflected in many stories, is submission to the glory of nature, reflecting Banerjea's own great love for the environment—oneness being an ultimate Truth. 'The Banyan Tree' lays out evocative descriptions of "man fusing into the folds of Nature" that take the reader to human-environment interface possibilities as yet unexplored. 'Bewitching Sundarban' introduces you to the majesty and magic of the "world's largest tidal delta". And 'Mahua Magic' has the reader envisioning a world in which an evening drink with a bear was part of daily routine.

Banerjea's career as an educator, her choice of thesis on women criminals of Bengal in the 18th and 19th centuries and her training in psychological counselling all equipped her to explore the many colours and triggers of agency. Readers of this collection will reap the benefit of her journey, via well-etched characters, tight plots and an authenticity that reflects the author's own agency to write: bringing alive protagonists who find the courage to fight the war within—and take flight. Banerjea makes it easy to fly with them.

Sushmita Ghosh
Former Global President of Ashoka:
Innovators for the Public from 2000–2005
Currently Ashoka Leadership Team Emerita
and Member of Ashoka's global board of directors

(Ashoka identifies, supports and connects social entrepreneurs who craft systemic solutions to society's intractable problems in more than 96 countries.)

1

Playhouse Park Street

I am Avasa, thirty-one years old. A nice ripe age, with the right balance of mellowness, texture and flavour. And true to my name, I am independent. Also free like the unbound tide, irrepressibly imaginative like a child's fantasy.

My parents were teachers, immersed in the routine of syllabus, classes, paper setting, corrections and back to the completion of the syllabus. The boring monotony of the stone grinder. I could hear the whirrrrr...rrr of the circling going round and round and.... Caught as they were in their concentric circles existence, they realised quickly enough that their progeny did not have it in her to go through the grrrr...ind of higher education. School was torture enough. The rigours of history, geography, maths left me petrified—a little like the victims in the *Harry Potter* books.

BUT...give me the bewitchment of theatre to get my limbs and mind galvanised into action. Even today. The opportunity of watching a play was and is bribe enough to get me to do the 'horriblest' of jobs. Let me give you an example.

I was in class six. A theatre group from Mumbai was visiting Kolkata. And they were putting up the play *Matilda,* based on the book by Roald Dahl. I was churning with excitement and the sheer anticipation of going to an auditorium to get transported to a wondrous world of magical powers. Anything could happen on stage—yes *anything*. Books, tables, chairs could move on their own just with that concentrated gaze. The bullies would be duly punished with Matilda's astounding mind power. And I could live out my fantasies through her as her magic would carry me to the enchanted world.

"Clear out your cupboard, complete the backlog of the maths homework and attend the family function if you wish to go for the play," boomed my mother's voice.

"Why?" I fumed inside. A function where some over-curious and over-interfering aunts and uncles would interrogate me with a billion questions about matters which were frankly none of their business. And to ensure that I got to go for the play I would have to answer them sweetly while seething within—"Why do you wear jeans with nearly torn knees? Show some respect. There are so many important guests in the gathering."

"Oh goodness! Such short hair, just like a boy. Don't you like being a girl? Your poor parents. How will they ever find a match for such a tomboy?"

How can I forget the trouble-maker, much, much older cousin I would have to make polite conversation with? She had sneakily taken my diary out of my drawer, read it and then reported all my secrets (written in rather angry language) to my mother, some of which were about the trouble I was having with my parents over my 'obsession' with theatre. Such betrayal! And all done under the veil of being the concerned and helpful niece to my mother.

"It is lucky that I found it and not someone else who would gossip. Be careful with your daughter. I am worried for you. She is far too rebellious and self-opinionated at such a young age. Her fixation with drama is unhealthy and unnatural. You need to control her."

She did not 'find' it. She stole it and needed to be taught to respect others' privacy. And who was she to talk about how I was to be brought up considering that her own creation had been suspended from school for unacceptable behaviour. "Set your own house in order before you pretend to be the good Samaritan setting the world right," I felt like telling her. Someday I would, in my own way.

In fact, I did. A few years later I found her one evening, holding hands intimately with a stranger in the corner seat of a restaurant. Out came my phone and I took a picture and sent it to her husband. You get the message, right? Don't mess with me. But to get back to my earlier story.

I did get to watch the play. And, eventually, went on to create my reality on stage at the theatre, Playhouse Park Street. My characters were free, unhindered by false notions of prestige, status and pretences of being well-wishers. Not for me the mundane existence of uninspired beings, creatures of habit and routine, limited by claustrophobic boundaries.

I flew, painted the sky, talked to translucent cloud nymphs about their misty adventures, embraced the exuberance and joy of Dasharathi's pranks on boastful characters (of Sukumar Ray's Pagla Dashu), lived and created the future with Satyajit Ray's Professor Shonku, taught the criminals a lesson or two with Premendra Mitra's Ghanada. And I chatted with Beatrix Potter while munching fresh juicy vegetables and sipping chamomile tea about the new escapades of Peter Rabbit in the garden (adding my own ideas about how he tricked McGregor) and also watched enthralled as E.H. Shepard lovingly brought to life A.A. Milne's loving, brave, comic, honey gorging, charming Winnie the Pooh.

You could of course pooh pooh it all away and say, "Bah! Imagination runs berserk. Get a hold on yourself and get back to the REAL world." But who gives anyone the right to decide what is real for me. My world exists and is authentic because I believe in it. A scientist is believed to have said that reality is merely an illusion, albeit a very persistent one. So! But never mind, I will not get trapped into the quagmire of this debate. I will merely proceed with my story.

Fortunately 'well-wishers' like my much, much older cousin could not influence my parents who let me be, with my books, ungovernable and illusionary reality and I took to the stage like a bee to its hive, creating my own elixir. Would it surprise you if I said that my hive also took to me, warming up to the comfort of a mutually interdependent existence? We lived as lovers do, immersed in each other, missing each other painfully when we were separated.

I remember my first serious performance when I was in my teens. It was a challenging role of a young, innocent girl pushed to the edge by circumstances and finally taking to guns and violence as the leader of a gang. It required me to delve into all my unexpressed magma of simmering emotions to gain the empathy of the audience as the play climaxed to a resounding gunshot. And even after the curtains came down I wept, emptying my chamber. It was my hive, my Playhouse, that took me into its fold, with its caressing and understanding touch, giving me the space and time to gather myself.

With time and my rendering of various roles, I picked up a reputation of being a talented artist. For me though, it was living the characters. I became them, could feel every feeling they were going through, predict what their responses to situations would be, use the words sitting on their lips and quite often say the lines I instinctively knew they were dying to say, which were not a part of the script handed over to me. Certain popular productions ran for several months, at the end of which it was a huge effort to find myself again.

You could call it an obsession or a true merging with the persona—but that is the way it was and is for me. When the platform comes live with the stage-lights and I stand under the sliver of light coming down, I look up and can experience all the artists who have performed before me, in the tiny sparks floating around. I can hear their voices, spot them in their costumes and feel their presence all around.

And so it was with late Kalpana and Rohit.

Known to the Kolkata stage as two of the greatest actors, the story of their tumultuous love affair was what I, Avasa, was enacting. The plot unfolded through a series of dialogues and I had the demanding task of playing both their parts.

As the play progressed and the conversation became more impassioned and heated, something happened... something inexplicable. I began merely voicing the words of a script alien to me...becoming the audio messenger of a story unknown and untold. I became the deliverer of a confession.

"Each time I came on the stage with you I felt afraid. It had never been like that, quite the reverse actually. Our natural chemistry had me melting in your arms. But I was losing my confidence."

"And you blame me for it, Kalpi? Me! I felt alive because of you, every free moment I had would be spent imagining our snatched minutes together, stolen from the prying eyes. I cannot believe that you are weaponising your fears and targeting the man who loved you with every cell in him."

"I felt frightened, Rohit—scared of the intensity of my feelings for you. You must understand that the fear of losing you made me insanely insecure and jealous. Losing you would mean that a part of me would die too. I could not allow that now, could I?"

"I don't understand. I remember our last night together. The care you had taken to make everything special—the perfumed pillows, flower petals on the bed sheet, your lace negligee, my favourite wines and your softness yielding to every move till we clung to each other, exhausted but hungering for more."

"Yes I wanted it to be memorable, for you and for me."

"Are you suggesting that you knew it would be our final goodbye?"

"Not suggesting, informing you. I had planned it that way. Did you never wonder why you suddenly took ill the next day and your heart gave way? What I had mixed in your wine did the trick. But the world was never the wiser for it. I am telling you today. An admittance you could say but who is going to catch a spirit, ha ha!"

"But why, Kalpi? I loved you so much. We could have had so many more years of bliss together."

"Don't you realise I did you a favour? Took you away while you were still at your peak. People remember you that way, even today. We are the eternal sweethearts of the Bengali theatre, the elusive enchanting beauty of youth."

"But you did not do it as a favour to me. That became the outcome of my untimely death. You had other things on your mind. I had sensed a desperation in you, even in our lovemaking on our last night but put it down to your being uncontrollably aroused. What was it?"

"Yes, you are right. It was not a planned outcome but that is the way it worked out for us. I was privy to the information that you had agreed to a contract with the starlet in her teens, the one who they said was my lookalike and would storm the stage with her performance. After all, mother and daughter could not both be your beaus—it is not acceptable in esteemed society. Do you remember our first night together? I was barely fifteen though I pretended to be older and experienced and you were my senior by quite a few years. A married man, much sought after."

"And, you are saying all this now? Are you suggesting that I am the father? I had a daughter and I did not even know. I feel so cheated and betrayed. You could not enjoy the adulation from your fans for long either. I now understand. The guilt of your act weighed on you and alcohol became your friend and eventually your foe."

"But we did have a good time while it lasted, did we not? It is not the quantity that counts but the quality, as is said. And you were protected from the slander of having an illegitimate child. And later, the possible entanglement with your own child. I took care to give her up to an orphanage. But when I saw her years later on stage, I just knew. After all, theatre runs in her blood. She could not help it. But I did not tell her. I simply watched her grow from the wings and eventually as a little floating spark in the spotlight that highlighted her on stage, I rejoiced in her achievements. That way my yearning to be on stage was also met."

"And now that we are both in the light world, we need to applaud and bless her through the stage lights, as she tells our story, her story, to the world."

I sat benumbed and anesthetised, by my own words. Words I had no control over, could not touch but words which had stroked, agitated and then frozen my very being. It was a revelation that would take me a long while to process. I had two sets of parents. How many people had that privilege? It was no wonder that the world of academics never appealed to me. The genetic tug of theatre won hands down.

Silence reigned in the packed auditorium. And then a deafening applause tore through the hundred-year-old hallowed hall. Were my birth parents being granted absolution, divine forgiveness through the vehicle of the very audience that had sat in judgement of their penance, the public acknowledgement of their startling lives? I will never know but can only hope that it was so.

And I sent up a prayer for the window or should I say light beam provided to me to unite with my parents in the realm that I know and love best—the miraculous playhouse of drama and theatre where just about anything can happen.

2
The Banyan Tree

The locals had conflicting stories about the tree. "It is said that even if you cut it, it grows back overnight."

"No, no, the truth is that if you cut even one branch the tree grasps the person."

There was mystery and awe surrounding it.

"I have heard that the tree breathes heavily when it gets angry," added the retired postmaster, who looked as gnarled and seasoned as the tree itself.

For me it was a fascinating study in architecture and design, of man fusing into the folds of Nature. A gigantic banyan tree stood in the middle of the house, with its multiple mile branches forming a verdant green canopy across all the eight rooms, most of which were locked. There were no other guests that night. Instead of bricks, logs had been used to divide the space into living areas. In place of a concrete or tiled roof, the ingenious architect had used a strong transparent material for the ceiling, which arched several feet above the tree. As dusk fell and sunlight was switched off, on came a zillion starlights in the green crown of my room. To say that I was starstruck would be an understatement.

The floor mimicked the red coarse soil of the region, without being corrosive to my bare feet. Some of the aerial roots had been trimmed, others had been camouflaged into hanging lights with wicker baskets and the older roots that gripped the soil had been used to form cosy alcoves with comfortable sofas made from bamboo. One slightly larger alcove was transformed into a mini bar.

'Canopy Hermitage' had been an abandoned property for over four decades. Lost in the wilderness of a jungle in North Bengal, it was discovered by an architect trekker. Delighted with his discovery and fuelled with an irrepressible spirit, he managed to navigate the reams of red tape to retrieve the magical creation from being lost forever. He surrendered to its charms and allowed his imagination the luxury of a wild canvas to play with. And the creation was enchanting.

Not widely publicised, this boutique hotel had been recommended to me by Arpan, my wildlife enthusiast friend. It was end February and the season was turning. The stark chill of winter was easing into the romance of blooms and birdsong. Arpan and I were chums from childhood and he could sense the unrest building up in me. Work pressure, burning embers of a broken heart and the weight of guilt and regret were the hot spots in me, waiting to erupt. The safety valves needed activation and so here I was.

"Spiritual upliftment will be assured as well as rejuvenation at an elemental level," Arpan assured me with a mischievous glint in his youthful eyes.

Intrigued, I asked, "I get the former going by the bottle collection you spoke about, but am a little apprehensive about the latter. Don't want my DNA messed around with. One never knows with you. The last trip we went on together had your psychic friend insisting that there was another me hiding inside me and would soon make its presence felt. Gave me the heebie-jeebies. I walked around for months in mortal distraught of suddenly finding a shadowy me walking alongside. What is this 'elemental' reshuffling all about? You better pre-warn me. As they say forewarned is forearmed. I am sure my basics are all nicely aligned and comfortable in each other's company."

"So you think. Just experience the place and then we will talk," was the enigmatic response.

"Provided of course the X and Y axis in my mind-body frame remain stable. As long as this is not one of your 'be one with universal consciousness' trips, I am curious to go and see this place. God knows I can do with a holiday."

"Just go and don't be so suspicious. I have no ulterior motives, trust me. It will be an experience of a lifetime, one that your great-grandchildren will also want."

Arpan's offer was enticing, had the promise of being deliciously different and I was in the mood to be seduced. A recent reading echoed in my tired brain, "let your guards down, be vulnerable and the truth will be revealed".

As evening deepened and the jungle sounds became more pronounced, I shut the windows of my room and walked into the living room which had a dining table on one side. The slab of wood was balanced on the root of a tree with its rolling muscular limb sitting on the floor. The beauty was striking. On the table was a book that I was drawn to. It was all about the *panch maha bhutas*—the five organic foundational building blocks—both inside us and the world around. Keeping these in harmony and balance and spring cleaning them was the recommended route to a joyful state of existence. Curiosity overtook me. Was I on the path to renewal at the elemental level? Is this what Arpan was hinting at?

I had been introduced to the concept of five natural elements but had not visualised myself being a concoction of air, water, earth, fire and space or ether. It was fine to have them existing in the geographical world—but a trifle disconcerting imagining myself as raging fire, gushing water, whooshing wind, muddy earth and infinite space. The lines, "All are from the dust, and to dust all return," seemed very real now.

The living room was large and in one corner was a welcoming fireplace. There was a chill in the air and the fire had been lit. Around it were large sofas with hand-rests. The sofas had been designed keeping the natural contour of the wood. The raw, rough appeal matched the ambience of the room as did the floor. 'Lal mati' or red earth was the signature draw of the region. It was not just beautiful to look at—it also emanated charm, solidity and foreverness and as I walked around barefoot on the red earth I felt a sense of grounding and rooting. Urban life had robbed me of the touch with unadulterated soil and grass and here the soles of my feet were soaking in pure and abundant energy, charging me.

The cook had laid out a simple and wholesome meal made with the local produce and what was grown in the hotel garden. Oil and spices were sparsely used and there was crunchy freshness in every bite. Thoroughly satisfied and satiated, I decided to warm my insides before retiring for the night. The fireplace beckoned. Armed with the book about the *maha bhutas,* I made myself comfortable on a sofa, read a bit about the element of fire and looked at the flames, crackling and dancing to a tune I was not privileged to hear. But there was a rhythm and I found myself responding to it. The fire in me, the life spark was talking to its kindred spirit and I became an observer, almost watching a replay of the recent emotional upheaval in my life. Fire illuminates, is a driving force and a source of confidence. It is capable of putting us on the highest gear of self drive. Yet, the same fire can consume us, singeing the delicate, soft and subtle textures.

I had experienced both. More recently the latter. Hungry for power and impatient to acquire it quickly I had played dirty politics. I had cooked up false allegations against my colleague who I sensed was the greatest hurdle in my path. The planning had been carefully done and greed and envy are powerful accomplices. I had used my fire, my unbridled passion for control, negatively, and succeeded in my game plan. The steps on the ladder to success were quickly climbed but there was no sense of fulfilment. Other colleagues had sensed that something wrong had been done but could not charge me with evidence. They merely avoided me. And my girlfriend of over seven years became wary of me. There was fear and mistrust in her eyes and the distance between us grew. I knew I had lost her and it made me wild and unbalanced with grief and regret. But the dye had been cast.

The rekindling of these feelings of desperation rushed to my lungs, throat and head and there was almost an orgasmic explosion, minus the pleasure. And then there was a calm. It was tiring but there was clarity. I knew what I had to do to balance the flaming fire within me. Getting some paper and a pen I wrote to the company head, resigning from my post and confessed about what I had done. I also wrote to my girlfriend apologising for what I had put her through. The third letter was the most difficult to word. It was to my colleague whom I had wronged. All three letters were put in envelopes with the addresses and sealed. The cook promised to post them the next morning. I had also emailed them but the internet connection being weak, I was not sure if it would work. I did not want to take any chances. The raging fire had almost died down in the fireplace as had the burning inside me.

The long journey, fire revelations and the sumptuous meal all contributed to a need for stretching out and falling into slumberland. Changing into my comfortable night attire, I stumbled into bed. The room was lit by the glow of the stars twinkling in vast open space. I breathed as deeply and richly as I could and gazed up. The light cast shadows as it made its way through the lattice of leaves and the beauty was numbing. Staring up I could sense a feeling of soaring freedom, almost as if my mortal being was being transcended into the caress of infinity. I was one with the limitless, boundless energy around me. The minuteness of my existence was clearly evident as was the burden of anxieties that I had been lugging around. There was relief, gratitude and relaxation as my tears flowed freely, releasing the pressure and pain.

Dawn broke through the leafy sky, with rose-coloured diamond dewdrops sparkling in the fragile sunbeams.

Even the magnificent power of Nature seemed vulnerable at this hour. I was eager to embrace it.

The previous evening and night had been eventful—scrambling my insides—yet had left me with a sense of serenity. I was now ready to deal with the wind and water. Two-thirds of me was water, gurgling and splashing around and without breath there was no life. The fresh misty morning air settled damply on my face. Lustily, I sucked in nosefuls and mouthfuls of this nectar, filling the cavity of my chest. I was breathing in the hope and promise of a clear new day, just breaking, and expelling all the sludge sitting inside, heavy and opaque. Spring was in the air and the cleaning was happening. The churning was in progress.

There was in me a growing eagerness to know a little more about this unique spot and the banyan tree. What was the story behind it if there was any? Was there anyone who could give the 'authentic' details and not just the weaves that had been concocted in the mind looms of the locals? I asked the staff at the hotel and after an exchange of furtive glances, on my repeated requests, they directed me to the hut of a wizened old woman.

She lived by the banks of a jungle stream burbling through the foliage, close to the hotel. She had the reputation of being a magic healer, who spoke the language of animals and plants and was intimately acquainted with the properties of any climber, shrub or tree. I was both sceptical and intrigued. Trampling through crunchy dry fallen-leaf beds and squelchy patches of slippery earth, I finally found her puffing into a mud caked *chulha*[1] to blow life into the fire made with dry branches.

Her clear penetrating blue eyes shone through her creased and wrinkled face and peered at with me with the intensity of a high wattage electric current. Without my asking she said, "So what makes you think that there is a story behind the tree? And why are you so interested?" She was speaking in English and that was even more intriguing.

"Every historical ruin has some story to it and this is a living testament to history. I don't know why but I feel very drawn to the tree. I respond to it almost at an organic level. And how do you speak such good English?" I asked.

"My grandfather taught it to me. He had learnt it from a young English 'seeker'." And then she paused and scrutinised my face again, closely, and I could see a flurry of emotions flitting across her face, almost as if she was having an internal dialogue. Then her features settled to a placid state.

"You may or may not believe what I am about to reveal but this is what my grandfather told me. He was a man gifted with special powers and aspiring ascetics would come to him to get his blessings and learn about the path to salvation. So had this young man from the West who was drawn to the mystical East. He became my grandfather's *shishya* (pupil) and stayed with him, helping him in his daily chores. My mother, Jayanti, a young spirited woman and he would share the work and

---

[1] Handmade village oven made with bricks and clay.

study from their guru. With time, along with spiritual awakening, their sensual world was aroused too. They came to love each other deeply. My grandfather was an understanding man and told me that he had a difficult time getting them to concentrate on their lessons. They had eyes only for each other and all their waking and sleeping hours they were together. And then I happened."

I was hooked to her story. The romance was an added dimension and I was eager to know what followed.

"Their joy knew no bounds and my father cared for her in every way he could, from cooking for her, washing her clothes and ensuring that she was not burdened in any way. The story however did not end as 'living happily ever after'. It was a very difficult delivery and my mother did not survive it. The world had ended for my father. My mother was buried next to a banyan sapling and I became my grandfather's responsibility. In some strange way, my father blamed himself for her passing and resolved to do penance by sitting by her grave and meditating."

Not prepared for this turn to the narrative I sat quietly for some time, sharing her grief. She continued, "I was told that my mother was striking to look at—skin like polished mahogany, hair like the cascading waterfall, laughter that tinkled across the valley and her mind was as sharp as lightning. My father was tall, his sun-bronzed body rippled like the sinews of a charging tiger and his face was kind and luminous with eyes like the blue ocean."

There was more to the story. "Nothing and no one could persuade my father to break his meditation. The seeker in him had taken over his mind and body. My grandfather soon understood that it was pointless trying to distract him, respected his decision and let him be. In him he had seen a purity that was rare. Tales of his charm and beauty had spread far and wide and many young women too tried to woo him away from his single-minded pursuit of salvation. He simply sat at that spot and was lost in *dhyana*[2]. The banyan sapling grew into a tree and wound its branches around him, making him a part of its being.

Both nourished each other—the tree was blessed with his divinity and he got a secure home. He had reached the level of *sadhana*[3] where nothing could touch him and he could achieve his own *mukti*[4] from the worldly bindings. The vibrant tree became his eternal physical abode."

"Wait," I asked her. "Are you saying that he just meditated and breathed his last inside the tree, the one inside the hotel and his mortal remains became a part of it?"

"Does that surprise you? Don't worry. He had no bodily sensations by then. That is the way he willed it to be—next to his Jayanti. Now would you like to see where the lovers collected water from as they went about their daily routine life?"

"Yes, I would," I agreed readily. The story was compelling enough for me to do a time travel and try and see what life was like for them. The old lady walked to

---

[2] Deep meditation.

[3] Spiritual realisation.

[4] Release.

the stream with her earthen pot and I followed her, lost in thought. There was a strange sensation surging through me. She dipped her feet and the pot in the crystal clear water and urged me to do the same. "Water has nurturing and healing qualities. It's relaxing power allows us to balance our emotions and get in tune with our feelings. Water washes away our fatigue, tension and even our sins and do you know, we believe that water has memory. It absorbs and retains the emotions we communicate to it. It can reveal hidden messages." Saying this she stepped away.

Slowly I walked up, gingerly dipped my toes in the sparkling, cold water and looked down. Staring back at me, in the reflection was a bare bodied, tall, young man with sun-bronzed skin, rippling muscles and eyes as blue as the ocean. Standing alongside was a startlingly attractive woman with skin like polished mahogany and hair like a cascading waterfall. "I've been waiting so patiently for you. What took you so long?" she said and cradled her arms into mine as her carefree laughter tinkled across the valley.

3

Mahua Magic

We were driving on a highway in eastern India. It was a large vehicle, eager to swallow miles and ride the free flowing feel of the moment. Spring was bursting with life and promise all around us and we, a bunch of college students, responded with full throated songs of the magic of love. One had recently been introduced to it and was in a state of euphoria; a couple, after the initial hello and a long handlock...errr...liplock were suffering from the aftertaste of sour grapes; and the rest, except one, were tremulous in the bubble of anticipation. The 'except one' was sceptical and voiced concerns about the consuming power, one way or the other, of this mysterious sentiment. It was a curious mix of perspectives.

Along the road were the famous mahua trees and we were soaked in the fragrance of the mahua flowers. "This trip will be a complete waste if we don't get to taste the mahua drink brewed by the tribals. They make it from the flowers and the getting high factor is pretty potent. The Brits too were well versed in this subject. Just look at the flowers, man! Strewn all around. It is like a bed of joints[1] waiting to be, in this case, distilled and consumed," said an excited Rakesh.

"Hold it, hold it. I get your unquenchable anticipation but I certainly don't want to be behind bars for buying

---

[1] Rolled cannabis cigarette.

mahua wine of all things. In certain states it is illegal to brew this in case you didn't know. And, historically it has been the cause of ruin for many because of widespread alcoholism," cautioned Satyam.

"You have the unique ability to be the soggiest of blankets to douse the raging-est of fires. An ideal candidate for the fire department. You have your career chalked out, man. I was told this poor man's drink, if smartly packaged and advertised, could easily be on the top ten best seller chart worldwide. Imagine that and here we are missing this electrifying opportunity," replied a petulant Rakesh.

"Bro, you are not alone in your desire for floral intoxication. Sloth bears will give you a run for your peg. They are known to munch on mahua flowers for the kick. And, by the way, these trees have multiple other uses too. The fruit, seeds, bark and even the timber—are used for medicinal purposes and for making rough furniture. We could console our spirit buds with mahua laddoos which are much in demand I've been told," informed Vignesh, the quiz expert.

The occasional verbal bantering continued and Hindi film songs on the journey of togetherness and bonhomie now became the chosen theme. Vivid images of Amitabh Bachchan and Dharmendra riding and singing together, professing undying friendship in the film *Sholay*, found another life. We were entering a wooded area and the winding road, cooled by the shade of the mahua trees in the afternoon sun looked and felt inviting. "Open clear roads, the scent of the forest, the occasional sparkle of sunbeams through the leaves, the cool breeze, the soft earth on the sides carpeted by flowers—what better place than this to take a break over our stock of sandwiches and coffee," declared Rakesh, the incorrigible adventurer.

The idea found immediate agreement with us friends and Devansh at the wheel looked out for a good spot to stop the car. As he manoeuvred a bend in the road he felt a palm clasping his shoulders in a tight grip from the back. Vignesh, who was sitting on the backseat and known for his keen eyesight, held on to Devansh and with whispered urgency asked him to slow down. "Look ahead. Stop the car here. I have to take a photograph. It is one of those once in many lifetimes moment."

It was a sight to behold. On Nature's mahua flower bed lay a bear and a man, embracing each other, the man's face nestling in the beast's hairy chest, his leg comfortably cushioned on its belly, both united and lost in the bliss of mahua magic. The gentle rustling of the leaves in the soft wind that blew over them was the Creator's lullaby.

Care was taken to not disturb the sweet ecstasy of the blithe spirits, floating around in never-never land. Memories were frozen in videos and pictures of the extraordinary sighting. "Oh, how I wish I could exchange places with the man for just a little while to experience the insouciant outlook to life—no worries, no troubles, no responsibilities—free of and unconfined by fears and norms to hug a mighty wild animal. How peacefully they both sleep," said a trance-stricken Rakesh.

"Not to forget that the wild animal too is 'unknowest' of its natural instincts in this state of inebriation. Sloth bears are not exactly the friendliest of creatures. Quite the contrary actually. They are known to be very dangerous and aggressive. Our man better wake up from his stupor long before his mahua-induced friend and beat a hasty retreat if he knows what is good for him. Am sure he does, given that he is a local," warned Satyam, the vigilant, balanced one in our circle, clipping wayward wings that threatened to sprout every now and then.

Rupam, the quiet one in our band of brothers, with an understated sense of humour, spoke up. "This reminds me of a story an uncle of mine recounted when we were visiting a tea estate in North Bengal. He is an old hand in the tea business and cannot stay away from the hills for any length of time. The incident happened in the early years of his career. As you all know the burra bungalows of the burrasahibs, the estate managers, are a throwback to another era—spacious, well ventilated rooms with high ceilings, wooden floors and majestic wooden staircases, verandahs circling the main building, the kitchen and bakery behind the house from which wafted the most tempting of aromas, bountiful kitchen gardens for fresh herbs and fruit laden trees in the impressive gardens. And, of course, how can one forget the retinue of house help for the upkeep, the spit and polish shine and the divine spread on the dining tables. I too was privileged to experience a slice of it during my visit."

"Okay, okay, enough of your reminiscences and meanderings. Either you promise to invite us to your uncle's paradise and then we will listen to some more of your literature or just get on with your core story," remarked an impatient Rakesh.

"Perhaps we could have both. My cousin, his son, now works in a tea garden," smiled Rupam enigmatically and continued, "As I was saying, my uncle was a fresh recruit and had been invited by his boss for dinner to his bungalow. It was late autumn and a nervous young lad went across in the evening. Temperatures had dipped and a crackling fire had been lit in the drawing room. My uncle surveyed the finer details of the carved furniture, the paintings and the select curios, imagining his time as the big boss. He made himself comfortable on the sofa upholstered in a pastel paisley design, close to the glowing teak staircase with polished handrails, leading to the upper floor.

The gracious host and hostess offered him the choicest of drinks and a variety of juicy kebabs as starters. Another couple joined them and conversation flowed from one anecdote to the other, all related to amusing happenings in the estates. It was a world by itself.

A couple of drinks down, when there was a slight lull in the conversation, my uncle's attention was drawn to some movement on the staircase. In the diffused light he saw a large shaggy creature ambling down. He blinked hard and gradually shifted from a relaxed stance to an upright spine. The hosts were now involved in a discussion with the other guests and my uncle seemed to have lost his voice.

And he had good reason for this. It was a huge bear that was nearly at the foot of the stairs and seemed to be focused on an open cauldron placed on a table close by, next to the hat stand. Very much at ease, the animal headed straight for the bowl and drank its contents. By now my uncle had regained sketchy control over his vocal chords and in a quivering tone, pointing at the beast, asked his host, 'W…w…what is g…g…going on?'

The gentleman and his wife laughed indulgently at his discomfiture and assured him that everything was in order. The bear was a resident of the house and had come down for his evening drink. It was a measured amount that was kept for it. Having had his fill, the family member then trundled into the drawing room, made himself comfortable on a cushion that obviously belonged to him, gave a casual disinterested look around and as the drink started taking effect, shut his eyes and dozed off. For my uncle of course, the impact of all the connoisseur's liquor he had consumed, had bid a hasty adieu and the night seemed immeasurably long till dinner was served and he could take his leave to go back to the sanctity and sanity of his humble quarters."

We were all assimilating the story when Rakesh came up with his observation. "Bro, on second thoughts, maybe the visit to the burra bungalow is not such a great idea after all. Don't think I have the liver to share my evening drink and sweet nothings with a wild animal. Perhaps it is a question of being in fine tune with nature but don't think I have evolved enough as yet. Need more time."

Vignesh, our window to the world, put his mind at rest. "No tension on that front. There is now a law in India pertaining to a long list of animals including bears that cannot be kept as pets. This story belongs to a bygone era. Our hopes of a tryst with the good life, even for a few days, remain alive. Mists, mighty mountains, magical mansions—here we come."

Rakesh heaved an exaggerated sigh of relief as our car sped across the road. Life's journey promised to be an interesting one. It was getting to be late evening and Satyam, the ever cautious one, suggested, "Why don't we stop for the night in a hotel? The road seems pretty deserted and there are woods all along. Don't fancy getting drunken bear hugs in pitch blackness in case we have a car breakdown."

"Trust you to strip life down to the bare impossibilities. Here we are, drooling in the dream of delectable kebabs, fantasising about our fanciful stay in a burra bungalow and you bear doze it all with your ominous predictions," countered Rakesh.

Devansh, vigilant at the wheel, agreed with Satyam. "The misty fog from the hills is closing in and visibility has become a challenge. Next we will have translucent apparitions floating along our car. Too risky for my nerves," he added.

"Looks like we are in luck. There is an old palace turned hotel on this route. The mountain is the backdrop, like a cyclorama. Looks charming," informed Vignesh, quickly doing an internet search.

Decision taken, we peered through the lengthening shadows, on the lookout for our one-night palace home. The striking silhouette of the arched gate against the warm pink-toned sky caught us unawares. We stared. In awe. In silence. The hotel exuded a lost charm—out of a sepia-toned, yesteryear's movie. We were greeted by white, gold and maroon liveried men and they escorted us to a suite on the first floor, complete with a huge terrace overlooking a wild garden.

Time had forgotten to tick in the vast, slightly musty rooms. Huge beds with burnished brass posts on the four corners, sunken sofas with shabby brocade furnishing which seemed to have shaped themselves to the posterior of a rather large person, a table with a cut glass lamp which had glistened in times gone by and a huge mirror, the tiny self-cracks of which held images, in secret, of innumerable residents who had stayed in the room. I hesitated to see my reflection, lest I too became a prisoner in the crevices of the glass that appeared to be keeping vigil on the happenings in the room. A faint shiver quivered down my spine.

We were all sitting down to have a cup of tea when Rakesh declared, "I will have a hot bath in the ceramic bathtub and sprinkle the bath salts provided. Can't miss the opportunity to live the maharajah life, even if it is for one night, right?"

"At the rate you are going I won't be surprised if you demand your personal *dewanji* to take care of your fortunes," added Rupam.

The geyser was non-functional and we were asked to use the immersion heater, the likes of which I had seen in my grandparents' house. It had been a long day and the tea and stretched legs were having a soporific effect. Eyes half closed, we were enjoying long moments of tranquil bonhomie when Rakesh stepped out of his bath, exuding fragrant steam and a startling question.

"Who was this lady you all were talking to? She sounded British and you were having an animated conversation. I heard just a few words like 'croquet', 'martini' and 'fox trot'. Are you all planning an English ball?"

"The ambience is playing games with your head, boss. Next you will imagine Lord Mountbatten shaking your hand and briefing you about the future of India. Get a hold over yourself, man. We will enjoy our stay and be gone tomorrow, back to the grind," retorted Vignesh. Rakesh tried hard to convince us of his 'heard' experience only to be clamped shut by our joint denial.

Not convinced by us, Rakesh decided on going for a walk with Devansh, Satyam and Rupam. Vignesh wanted to take a shower and I stretched myself on the diwan. Lulled into half sleep by the peace in the room, I was woken by the sound of a knock on the door. It was an old, partially bent, liveried bearer who had brought in some candles and a match box—to be used in case there was a power cut.

"Huzoor, please excuse my disturbing you but now that you are up why don't you go to the terrace? The lights are on in the garden and you can see and hear the stream flowing by. Our guests love this."

His quiet melodic tone got me interested. Bobbing his hand between his forehead and torso he led me to the open space and I followed him, drawn by a hypnotic charm. It was wondrous. Twinkling roof, the sound of water lapping on the grassy stream edge and the fireflies flitting around overwhelmed me as I walked behind the old man. "The light from the room can cast intriguing shadows," I thought to myself, as the leaves of the wizened trees swished in the light breeze. "And my guide has such a benign smile," I noticed, following him unquestioningly as he kept looking back, engaging with me with his wrinkled eyes.

"Where the hell do you think you are going? STOP, stop immediately," shouted Vignesh, shrill panic in his voice. Shaken out of my trance, I halted. "I w…was simply following the m…m…man," I stuttered.

"WHICH man?" asked Vignesh as he came running, yanking me towards him. In the black space there was no man in front of me. I was standing at the very edge of the terrace where the wall had given way.

Life was certainly interesting.

4
Payeli

Payeli loved music. Even as a child, she insisted on wearing *payel*[1] with little silver beads that jingled to the beat of her tread. Sometimes she would take a little half-step, following it up with a double-step, and then she'd raise her foot and jiggle her feet—tolling her bells, announcing her arrival, 'tinkling' her little world. And thus she got her name, fondly given to her by her grandmother.

As she grew a little older, a music teacher was arranged to 'train' her. He sat her down and asked her to follow him, copying his notes, to be his dutiful *shishya*[2]. "I am your guru and your duty is to do exactly as I say. Where ever you sing later, people must know immediately that you are *my* pupil. There is no place for individuality here."

Payeli's feet itched to jingle her freedom, bound by no strict rules, collared by no *ragas*. They longed to sing freely, but Guruji would have none of it, and Payeli's dancing toes slowly lost their will. They were tamed, as was her voice, which hit the notes but forgot to sing the song of the soul.

---

[1] Anklets.

[2] Student.

"She has a voice that is in *sur*[3], but her songs are not *surili*[4]," was the verdict of her teacher. "She has no future and teaching her is a waste of my time and effort."

Dampened by his words, the family elders decided to discontinue the training. Payeli tried explaining her need for a different style of teaching, but her voice was cut short with, "You don't need to learn any more. This will not be a career for you, and the exposure needed has been given. Guruji has handled enough students to know what he is saying. Besides, you will get married anyway."

Case closed.

Music had given her wings to fly, and now she found the sky snatched away from her. And so Payeli lived. No, not lived, merely breathed her days until matrimony relieved her family of her.

Oh yes! The few lessons had enabled her to hit the right notes in her 'bride assessment' session. The investment had paid off.

Marriage took Payeli to the district town of Khanpur in Bihar. Her husband, an engineer, worked in a production unit of mica. They lived in a large house with the name 'Symphony' etched deep into the solid pillars at the gate. It had unkempt grounds and a barrack-like structure of 'outhouses' at a distance. Payeli loved the tranquillity of the garden, the tangled bushes, the mango-laden trees, and the curious and unfearful visits by birds, who came to her verandah to peck at biscuit crumbs.

---

[3] Tune.

[4] Tuneful.

The early mornings were her favourite time of the day. An early riser, she would quietly slip out of the huge, four-poster bed, and putting on a dressing gown, make her way to the garden. The millions of crystal clear dew drops, shimmering on the verdant green grass, lured her to walk barefoot on the lawn. The cool water drenched the soles of her thirsty feet, and the eastern sky, glowing with the promise of a new beginning, transfused its warmth into her being.

She felt mystically alive, listening to the call of the various birds, as they heralded the start of another day. Sometimes she would mimic the call of the persistent *koyel*[5] and at other times the eagle, whose call did not match up to its size. It was a game she played with them, trying to make her call as authentic as possible, to get into a calling match with the birds, when they answered her. She laughed to herself, playing with the mongoose in the garden or the large birds that would come to fish, in the lily pond, in one corner of the garden.

As soon as her husband left for work, she had her 'palace' to herself. She queened over it.

Her husband was a good man. Their interests however differed widely. "I find your passion for music and your love for the outdoors amusing and charming. Your eyes sparkle when you talk to the gardeners about planting some unusual flower. And when you listen to music you get lost in some other world," he observed.

With a happy smile she replied, "Yes, true, I love doing both. I am also happy you have friends here with whom

---

[5] Cuckoo.

you can play tennis and enjoy your game of Bridge. That way we can both do the things we like."

She cooked well and looked forward to it, thinking of the menu, organising ingredients, getting her assistant to grind the *masalas*[6] and then tempering the dish with her final touch. After years, Payeli once again felt the urge to sing in the freedom of her own space.

That morning was special. The hot and sultry summer sunbeams had been sprinkled with a shower and as she pottered around her spacious kitchen, a cool breeze, fragrant with fresh rain, wafted in. Payeli's spirits lifted and she broke into a song.

Unaired and unscrubbed, her 'singing' chords were initially reluctant to respond to her desire. Slowly, with repeated attempts, she finally coaxed them to get into tune.

Her 'soliloquy' song carried in it all her repressed emotions of pain, hurt, anger and rebellion along with a touch of '*abhiman*[7]'. The notes blew out of the window and rode the wind, travelling into the world outside, carrying her innermost self with it. So deeply lost was she in her song that she almost missed the drumming that had joined her notes. And then, almost unconsciously, she responded to the beat, quickening her '*taal*[8]'. "W...w...

---

[6] Spices.
[7] Hurt pride.
[8] Tempo.

what is happening? Where is this coming from? Who, who is it?" Questions swirled in her mind.

The drumming picked up tempo, too, and Payeli held her note—desperately trying to hold on to that moment in time.

There was something inexplicably magical about that instant. So she clung to it, afraid it might desert her. And the moment answered her silent plea, supporting her, almost like a wave on the shore, holding on to the poignancy of the split second before it surrendered to the coast. Payeli's being was carried to that shoreline, so fragile against the unleashed power of the ocean, yet defying nature itself as time stood still, applauding her music.

The moment passed and the sheer euphoria distracted Payeli. As she sang, her '*taal*' broke. Her voice faltered and mysteriously, the drumming picked up an insistent note, urging her to get back on track. Almost in a daze, she followed the beat and let the flow of her music ebb and rise, fasten and slow, to the call of the phantom tabla player.

She had unconsciously assumed that it was a man. Completely trusting herself to his call, she did not even question the presence of the tabla player, or ask around about what or who it could be. She had rediscovered her wings and was soaring into the sky. This time the sky was in her keeping with no threat of it being denied to her.

Payeli fiercely guarded the secret of her 'friend', even from her husband. 'He' made himself audible only to her, it seemed, and she was content with the arrangement.

He was there for her whenever she was ready to sing, and together they made music, like lovers complementing each other's most intimate and sensual moves. Entwined, her voice and the tabla made love with their music, giving each other pure ecstasy. As Payeli reached the climax of a *raga,* she could feel her heart and the tabla thudding against her eardrums. It was orgasmic in its intensity, a feeling entirely new and thrilling to her.

Whenever she slipped up, the tabla chided her, sharp in its note of disapproval for allowing her standard to fall. Autumn gave way to winter and then the cold warmed to the colour of spring. Payeli's songs changed moods with the seasons but her date with her companion remained evergreen, ever youthful, ever fresh. So happy was she that her joy bloomed out of her eyes, her smile and the very pores of her skin.

Payeli had heard whispers surrounding the history of 'Symphony'. Going by the hushed tales, the name should have been 'Unfinished Symphony'. Eager to know more, she located a book entitled, *The Ghosts of Khanpur*. And sure enough, she found a reference to their cottage.

There was one bit that caught her attention. "A *memsahib*, besotted by a young, handsome tabla player, had invited him to stay in one of the outhouses and accompany her while she sang and played the piano. With a stern and harsh man for her husband, she hoped to find a balm in the companionship of the young man, as well as nourishment for her love of music. Her creative zeal was to merge the music of the east and the west.

Things went fine for a while. They even got around to composing some original fusion pieces. The fusion, however, did not stop at music and the master soon got wind of the goings-on. The writing of the symphony was aborted, as was the budding affair. The tabla player was reported missing one morning, never to be heard of again, and the *memsahib* could be heard singing plaintive songs until late into the night."

The spirit of the tabla player, it was said, visited the house, hoping to complete the unfinished symphony. The older staff, who had been working in the house for many years, claimed to have seen the two, walking hand-in-hand in the garden. The cook's wife, who was the most social and talkative of them all, whispered to Payeli in confidence, "I saw them during the last full moon. The image was like a translucent cloud. The memsahib was wearing a long frock and the Indian man was in a kurta and pyjama. Now, how can I tell you, but I have to because no one else believes me. They were sitting on the bench. She was on his lap and they were lost in their kiss. I almost felt as if I was intruding. I even heard them humming a song together. It was a different kind of song, in some other language."

Payeli was curious. A frown creased her forehead. What did he look like? Why had he played for her? Was he looking for something more in their unique relationship? The more she heard about the couple in love, stronger grew her curiosity. Was it simply a strong desire to put a face to her invisible, always there companion or *could* it be that there was a small spark of jealousy ignited in her about the 'other woman', the *memsahib*? Or was it that she was terrified of the prospect that if the two found the freedom to live and love in the other world and make music together, she would be abandoned?

But 'he' was hers. Payeli's. He was *living* in the present, through his heartbeat, his rhythm, his pure energy and they were making music together in the real world. He was alive through her, with her, in her. Why would he choose what was dead, a memory, a thwarted dream?

Payeli was distracted. Her mind was torn. The niggling doubt shredded her. "What can I do? Who will I turn to for comfort or for answers?" The mounting pressure of all her negative thoughts, triggered by her childhood experiences of rejection, made her sit in the verandah and hold her head in despair.

"Ask the source of the doubt, to clear your confusion," floated the advice, blowing in the wind.

"But how will I converse with the unseen, someone I don't even know?" she asked.

"Talk in the language you know best," was the simple answer.

Yes. She could sing out her worries and her queries. That was what she knew best. That was her safe place, her comfort zone. So she sang out her questions aloud, releasing it to the universe, and waited anxiously for some response.

"Will you remain with me
Be my musical consort?
Are you happy to just be
Together with me, holding fort?"

The tension of the delayed response jangled her frayed nerves to snapping point. When the flame of her anxious hope, was flickering to a dying ebb, she heard the beat. First softly, and then with confidence. The notes spoke to her in the secret code between them. It was set to a rhythm.

"Music we will make together

My partner, no worry, no fear

Hail, storm or sunny weather

By your side I am, my dear."

The gentle sweetness of the answer made Payeli's heart dance. The *memsahib* had her place and she had hers. And the two, even if they did meet, would complement each other. Her friend was striding two worlds with the magic of his music and there could come a time when the three together would harmonise their music to echo in different realms. Just the thought transported Payeli from despair to eager anticipation.

One evening, when some guests were over for dinner, her husband suddenly requested her to sing for them. Initially reluctant, Payeli gradually gave in, and then allowed her music to flow, her companion keeping time. The group was lost for words until one of them exclaimed, "She must perform outside. Everyone should experience this divine gift."

So Payeli got to perform on stage. All were invited, including her family. She refused offers of an accompanist.

The day arrived and she stood on the dais, holding the microphone close to her mouth. Dressed in a maroon and gold sari, she looked stunning, with an air of quiet confidence.

She shut her eyes, took a deep breath and set free her soul to make music with her soulmate, creating their own unmatched symphony.

5

The Deal

"Class 3A, line up. Take your library books. Time to go to the library to exchange your books."

Mrs. Pereira, the class teacher, was getting her bunch of boisterous eight-year-olds in a semblance of order before they trooped down to the library. Feverish activity charged through the hundred-and-ten-year-old classroom as little hands rummaged through books in the much-handled teak desks. Some dived into the canvas school bags to pull out the *Jataka* Tales, Ruskin Bond, Enid Blyton and the like.

Library was a much-awaited class. Unadulterated fun. Dramatised story reading by the teacher, book browsing, and often an added treat, a video to watch. Ramesh had in fact brought along his favourite *Lion King* video for his classmates, as he had promised Mrs. D'Souza, the librarian.

The excitement was palpable, as thirty-odd boys got into the serious business of lining up. In the midst of all the activity, little Inder anxiously called out to his friend Russel, "Just wait for me. I can't find my book. Help me look for it." Russel was Inder's tiffin and Beyblade friend, and he quickly came back to rescue Inder. They were both aware of Mrs. D'Souza's temper, when it came to library books getting lost or misplaced. Two sets of hands plunged into Inder's desk and bag in a desperate search.

"Do you remember packing it?" asked Russel. "I'm not sure. I was very sleepy," replied Inder, his eyes filling up. A timid boy, he could not get himself to face what he perceived as Mrs. D' Souza's wrath. His father's blazing eyes, hurtful words and his mother's inconsolable sobbing and occasional shouting were familiar to him. As far back as his memory supported him. When alone with his mother he would hug her and they would find strength in each other. He trembled and his voice was a whisper. Besides, he had forgotten the book the previous week also.

"What are you two chattering about?" hollered Mrs. Pereira as she escorted the students out of the classroom. "Come quickly. There will not be enough time for all of you to exchange books if you delay the class."

In a last-ditch effort to save himself, Inder clutched Russel's hands and pleaded, "Will you please tell Mrs. D'Souza that you borrowed the book from me and forgot to get it? She will not get so angry, because you have your own book." Russel was not at all convinced, and his expression gave him away. Sensing that he was about to refuse, and before he could mouth the words, Inder pre-empted him and said, "Look I'll give you five rupees if you do this for me."

The words had been uttered and the deal had been placed on the table. Now he could only hope that Russel would be tempted to accept the offer.

Russel wasn't sure if he had heard right. "You will give me five rupees to save you? Where will you get it from?" he asked.

"My mother gave it to me. Look I am not lying," he replied, opening his pencil box to display his treasure.

"What on earth are you both doing? We don't have the whole day. You are delaying everybody," shouted Mrs. Pereira, impatiently. Before the deal could be officially closed, the two were bundled off to join the queue.

The boys started returning their books and took their cards to choose the next book they would issue.

"Inder Malhotra and Russel Mathew, may I have your books please."

Mrs. D'Souza's voice rang out loud and clear, and Inder clung to Russel's hand.

"Ma'am," said Inder, nervously, "Russel borrowed my book and did not get it today."

"And why, may I ask, have you forgotten his book, young man? I can see that you are carrying your book. It is selfish of you to deny him a new book to read this week. You have been irresponsible and there will be no new book for you," said the teacher, tapping her pencil menacingly on the table.

Russel, with all his life experience, could neither comprehend nor combat this charge. His quivering features collapsed, and tears rolled down.

"Oh stop whining and get on with your work. Crying is for the weak boys," said Mrs. D' Souza in a firm and unsympathetic tone.

The minutes were ticking fast, and the class had to finish the business of returning and taking books. The last fifteen minutes were reserved for watching the start of the *Lion King* video, and Mrs. Pereira promised the class that she would organise a special period for them to watch some more. The bell rang and the class walked out in single file. All except Russel and Inder. "Go on, go back boy, and stop sniffling," rebuked Mrs. D'Souza.

"Ma'am, I just wanted to tell you I did not take Inder's book."

There. The truth was out, and he felt relief. A startled Mrs. D'Souza glared at Inder who was also waiting with Russel.

Inder was equally startled. His deal had not paid off.

"So, what is the full story? I want to know the truth," asked a bewildered Mrs. D'Souza.

Timid Inder could no longer escape from the line of fire. He had faced the brute force of raw anger, and had seen it unleashed on others as well. Preparing himself for the worst, he looked tearfully at his teacher and, in a quavering voice, told her, "Ma'am, I was scared that you would be angry, so I told Russel I would give him five rupees if he protected me and saved me."

"What! Lying and bribing. Where did you get the money from, and how did you learn all this?" exclaimed a scandalised Mrs. D'Souza. In all her years of teaching, this was something she had not handled earlier. For once she was at a loss for words.

"Ma'am, I still have the five rupees that my mother gave me for keeping quiet and not telling my father that she had forgotten to pick up his suit from the dry cleaner. You see he beats her up very badly and that makes her terribly scared. So I thought that if I gave Russel the money he would keep quiet too, like I do."

"And you think this is the way to solve the problem? Every time there is an issue and you are frightened you will pay someone to do something wrong so that you are saved? What is it that you are most afraid of?"

"I wake up at night because of a dream where my father is drunk, I am being beaten with a belt and my mother's face is all swollen up and she is crying."

"Is it just a dream or have you experienced it?"

"I feel scared telling you. If my father gets to know there will be trouble."

It was a quiet and serious Mrs. D'Souza who took the matter up to the Principal. What were they to do? The initial contact was the mother who was terrified of her husband being brought into the picture. "Please do not involve my husband in this. He will beat me when he finds me alone at home, if he thinks his public image has been marred. In front of friends and in the office gatherings he behaves like a perfect gentleman. People think he is a kind and gentle person."

The Principal listened to her and then said, "So you are willing to allow this to continue? How does it help you by hiding this? Do you realise that your silence is enabling his behaviour? How long will you be able to keep it away from public notice? Would you like your son growing up like this? In class three he believes bribing is the normal way to handle things because he sees you doing it. He will face a serious clash between what he sees at home and what he is taught here. He is also psychologically traumatised because of the fear he has to live with day in and day out. You are a nervous wreck and in this condition what kind of parenting will you be able to do? You tell us what we can do under the circumstances.

We can advise you to find another school but that is not what we want to do. We need to find a solution to this."

"No, please don't ask me to go to another school. Inder's happiness comes from the friends he has made here. I don't want to snatch that away from him," begged the mother, reaching out to hold the Principal's hands.

"Neither do we," she replied, trying to comfort the mother. "But we cannot allow the present situation to continue either. We have a school counsellor who will help you and if necessary we will need to take the advice of a women's help organisation if he continues to abuse you. He is feeding on your fear. Such people are often cowards. Once you stand up to him and he knows we are there with you and Inder, I believe the situation will change. You have to help us. We are there to support you. Inder's welfare is primary for us. We cannot allow him to become a victim of circumstances not of his making."

After a lot of soul-searching and several counselling sessions, Inder's mother agreed to have the father brought to school. He had not been informed in advance about the reason for the parent-call. When asked by the Principal why his child was so scared and what his relationship with his son was, he replied promptly, "We bond very well and go out for fun rides and meals and I play cricket with him. Unfortunately, my wife is always stressed about his studies and marks and beats him up when he does not listen. She is extremely competitive and wants Inder to rank amongst the top three in class in every test. I think he is scared because of that."

"So, what you are saying is that Inder is very comfortable with you, looks forward to the good times that you have together and you are not overly anxious about his academic performance. It is his mother he is frightened of. We will have a joint meeting with the school counsellor, run a few tests and see how we can help Inder."

The family session was scheduled after a fortnight. The father was the epitome of consideration, kindness and compassion those fourteen days. "Inder, your mother is looking tired. How about giving her a break? Let us all go for a long drive and I will order some food. We can stop somewhere and have a picnic." He even joked about a mistake she had committed. "I thought I was the one who forgot to offer tea to a visitor. It seems she has caught my virus!" That made her even more wary. He took his son to the water-park and bought him a video game he had been asking for. He was convinced his game would pay off and his wife and child would not speak up against him in the session. Not going for the session would mean acknowledging that he was at fault and so was not willing to expose himself to questioning.

The day arrived and it was an affectionate father and husband who took the family to school. It was the mother who spoke first at the session. Her voice was calm and her manner confident.

"The past two weeks have shown me what a player my husband is. He has been exceptionally good to us assuming that we will be bowled over and forget his true colours. The truth is different. It highlighted to me that he understands what he normally does is absolutely unacceptable.

He also knows how to be considerate, affectionate and not controlling and abusive. I have decided that I will not allow this anymore. He thinks I am weak but I have got myself a job. If he raises his hands on either of us or verbally abuses us as he is so used to doing, I know whom to report the matter to. I have already spoken to them, so they are aware of the situation. My son will no longer be subjected to this vicious atmosphere at home. He will live the life of a child as is his right; in a caring, loving and nurturing home which I will provide by myself. I will be filing for divorce."

Inder looked at the new face of his self-assured and firm mother. No hunched shoulders or weak voice. She sat with her back erect and head held high, looking directly at her husband in the eye. It gave him solace and hope. Somewhere he understood that she would not cry inconsolably anymore.

He then looked at his father. It surprised him to see fear in his eyes—and...was he mistaken...sadness and tears? Too young to fully comprehend the ramifications of his mother's decision, he did know one thing—he wanted to be free of the feeling of constant threat and fear. He wanted to be happy. But did that mean throwing his father out of their lives? Wouldn't his father feel lonely? Divorce was a word he had heard mentioned and knew what it meant. A friend in his class had talked about his parents. He sat quietly and hung his head, not looking at anyone.

Initially, the father was at a loss for words and then tried to deny everything. The evidence of bruise marks meant he could not escape. His façade had been demolished. It was an aspect of his wife he had never seen earlier. He then tried to plead with her but was met with stony silence.

The Principal, who had been observing the proceedings, patted the seat next to her and spoke to Inder. "Come and sit next to me, my boy. Tell me what you feel."

Slowly Inder walked up to the chair and sat on the edge. He felt confused—was he happy that his father was being punished—was he relieved that his mother did not look terrified—was he sure he would not have to crouch under the bed when the shouting got too much?

"Tell me, Inder, what do *you* want?" came the gentle voice of the Principal, floating into his tired ears. "I want my father to say, 'Sorry, I will never scream or hit again. I will not come home angry.' And I want him to never do any of these things ever again."

"And if he does listen to you, what will you do?"

"I will ask my mother to give him another chance. Just like Mrs. Pereira gives us another chance to do the right thing if we are really sorry when we do something wrong. And if we make the same mistake again, then we are disciplined."

The Principal looked intently at the parents, giving them time to absorb what their child was saying.

6
The Eyes

The afternoon sun blazed, creating small, black, sticky pools on the tarred roads of Calcutta. I squish-squashed my way, down the arterial thoroughfare of the old dowager, the soles of my feet getting toasted through the burning rubber under the sandals. The golden haze hung like a giant shower curtain, compressing all the steam, and I willed myself to walk faster down the deserted street. Plip-plop, squelch-squalch, pish-pash—the music made by sweat and sticky shoe soles was my companion all the way to my destination—the grand old club building—as I hallucinated about the tall glass of chilled *nimbu pani*[1] with some *masala* strewn on top to add that extra zing.

Wiping my feet on the coir welcome mat at the entrance to the club, I stepped inside the foyer.

The striking white façade with the arches, tall ceilings, sweet scent of tuberoses, cool interiors and the soothing touch of the ancient marble slabs, alleviated some of the summer distress. But my parched insides craved that lemon drink, and I walked to the lift to get to the bar. The contraption was a relic, much like a lot of the city—both the structures and the living, who live in the past. The lift was a small one, and even two people brushed shoulders inside, as the engineering marvel shuddered up.

---

[1] Lemonade.

Reaching the lift, I found I was not alone. Standing in front of me was, for want of a more imaginative term, a relict! I got a rear view of the man: six feet tall, white breeches, polished black boots, a long, cut-away red coat with shining brass buttons at the wrists, white shirt, white wig with curls, fair skin, and an erect bearing. Was the man out of his mind? I was eager to know what he looked like. He would make an interesting subject for a painting.

Art was my calling and my forte was drawing portraits. Capturing the *being* of the person was my greatest thrill and I would spend hours studying the works of the world's renowned artists. Whether it was their impression of other people, caricatures or self portraits, I found it all deeply absorbing. There had been some well-known artists in my own family. Some even said that I looked like my great-grand-aunt, a professional portrait painter, known for her ability to penetrate her study and portray the essence on canvas.

He was probably shooting for a period film. After all, the City of Joy was a perfect location for such an endeavour. Or was he a member of the travelling theatre group that was in town? I could see no other members of the crew.

Perhaps he was the British connection in some advertisement in the making; it couldn't be a fancy dress, since that was a specialty of Calcutta in winter. My mind raced, searching for probable explanations, until the man turned around. It was a visual assault, in the suffocating heat. Piercing, blue eyes glared down at me from the irate face, as if to say, "How *dare* you come into *my* territory?"

Short of such abuses, every facial muscle was activated to communicate seething rage. I felt the unspoken words lash out at me and recoiled in anticipation.

The lift had come down by then, but I was not about to endanger myself by being in close proximity with this weird individual. Turning around hastily, I walked up the stairs to the first floor.

"Please make me the tallest glass possible of chilled *nimbu pani,*" I requested the bar man. He being the only person around at that time, I spoke half to him and muttered mainly to myself, "It almost seemed as if he believed he had proprietary rights over the club! Who on Earth did he think he was, behaving in this insolent manner?"

The incident stayed with me and so did the expression in his eyes. That evening, I narrated the episode to my family, but we couldn't come up with an acceptable explanation, though there was a lot of conjecturing.

"Perhaps you are being over-sensitive and reading too much into the situation," said my daughter.

"Maybe the man was thinking of something else, and had displaced his emotions on to you, who happened to be standing near him at that time," added my son.

"It could be he was getting himself into 'character', for a role he had to play," was my husband's opinion. Even wild imagination has some boundaries, and so we let the matter rest.

Two weeks later a group of us had gone to the club in the evening for a drink and were seated in a circle. The lounge still had the ambience of bygone days: large sofas, two layers of curtains (lace at the back and heavier furnishing in front), with scalloped edgings on the polished pelmet, shining mahogany centre tables with carved edges and legs, a bar made of Burma teak, white stucco work on the ceilings and portraits of eminent British men and women on the walls.

The tall grandfather clock struck nine. There was animated conversation, and we had new members joining us. The circle widened and as chairs were added to make room, I found myself sitting on the side facing the wall.

Conversation was flowing and all of us being members of the club, I commented, "Look out for some peculiar specimens walking around the club. I had a rather nasty experience the other day in front of the lift."

Someone who had his back to the wall asked me a question from the other side. "So, who was this man whose back you met in front of the bird-cage?"

I looked at him to answer, "It was one of those scenes like a remainder from the..." and a strangulated scream escaped my lips.

My eyes had strayed to the wall. Looking down at me from an ornate gold-gild framed painting on the wall was the very same face I had encountered in front of the lift! He was in the same outfit. The blue eyes were still glowering at me and saying, "*You* again, in *my* terrain!"

Obviously, my reaction made the group turn around to look at the painting. Puzzled expressions focused at me inquiringly. None of them found the appearance threatening. And yet, to me the piercing stare was terrifying.

Who was this man? Curiosity drew me to the club another morning, when I was by myself. Going up close

I read the name engraved on a small brass plaque under the frame. It was Mac Fross. The name rang no bell. The club archives did not have any details about him either. The National Library would be my saviour. And it was.

Mr. Fross was a very wealthy merchant who traded in spices and textiles from India and brought back precious stones and jewellery. He was brutal in his trade practices and amassed a huge fortune. Money had bought him status in society.

The book I had found had a painted portrait of him on the cover. It was in the lines of a biography and described some personal aspects of his life too. "Fross had everything he could ask for. A mansion, social standing as a successful businessman, all the worldly goods money could buy. But he missed a spouse. Unfortunately for him, his reputation as a ruthless master and a person with a vile temper, kept the ladies away.

The only persons who would strike up conversation with him were those interested in doing business with him. It was purely monetary transaction that they talked and then moved away. No one would invite him over for a meal or for some light-hearted conversation.

Fross grew lonely and bitter, making him all the more sullen. His surge to becoming fabulously wealthy, by his own wits, had also made him arrogant and he hoped to imprint himself in history through commissioning portraits of himself and paying people to write about his success.

There was an Indian lady, a Bengali, known to draw fabulous portraits, and he believed that only she would do justice to his looks and persona. Her steep charges made it all the more exclusive for him. What he had not bargained for, was, that in the course of the sittings, he would fall hopelessly in love with her.

Her name was Aparna Debi."

I was beside myself with excitement. So it was my great-grand-aunt who had drawn his portrait, the one on the book cover. The book also had a picture of her and it was true! I did look a lot like her. She must have been my age when that photograph was taken.

Eager to know how the story progressed I continued to read. "To spend more time with her, he commissioned three portraits, in three different outfits, drawn from three different angles. She could read her subject like an open book and though she drew the perfect paintings in terms of the posture, the feel of the rich textiles, the light and shade, she also captured the true inner look of the person. He did not look the confident, charming, gracious man he would have liked to be seen as. She caught his lost, lonely and bitter look.

But despite this, Fross was enraptured by her. Other than her professional charges, he gave her expensive gifts and went out of his way to win favour with her. He tried hard to kindle his softer emotions of love and compassion and try and impress her by donating generously to charities.

He attempted to cross the Bengali divide by studying Bengali literature and attending Bengali cultural events, knowing that these were close to her heart.

But his efforts were in vain. She knew him for who he truly was and refused him. Never having lost a challenge in business, he could not accept her refusal and went ballistic. The rejection was public knowledge and he could never live it down. It was rumoured that this spurning had possessed him, and even on his return to England, in his last days, he spoke of how he would make sure of winning her over, somehow. He died at the age of forty-five due to high fever."

The rest of the story was known to me as far as my relative was concerned. She had been betrothed to her husband at the tender age of fourteen and married him in her twenties and they had a very happy life together. In the family grapevine, I had heard stories of a *Saheb*[2] who had pursued her relentlessly but she had declined him. She had become the talk of the town but had handled it with dignity and grace.

Mr. Fross's dissatisfied and tormented soul obviously saw in me his thwarted love, since I resembled her a lot. All his pent-up pathos of unrequited love spilled over onto me. It was the reason why only I was privy to his dagger looks. Now that I knew the story, I actually felt sorry for this unhappy man.

The next evening, I visited his portrait once again, and when no one was looking, whispered, "I understand your pain and am sure you will find someone who loves you as much. I have immense faith in my prayers and am going to the church right now."

Did the expression soften a little? I am convinced it did!

As twilight drew the curtain on the last flicker of daylight, people found a candle glowing brighter than any other in the churchyard.

---

[2] Foreigner.

7

Swimming Along

Steamy, sweltry, sticky, stifling, August afternoons can be a sure-shot recipe for grouchiness and temper-on-the-edge-ness. I thought so too till I had my swimming adventures.

Mintu was the seasoned man in charge of the dressing room. Over two generations his family had mastered the art of—"man in the altogether"—management. Many a, shall we say, delicate situation had been manoeuvred skilfully by them. But on that day, even Mintu was challenged. In all probability, he hollered a desperate cry to his ancestor to come with some divine help.

Mr. 'X', let's call him that, is a rather large specimen of humankind who has difficulty pouring himself into his clothes and hopes like hell that the attire will find its own nooks and crevices to settle into. Born into a well-off family and being a prized boy-child, he has had to do precious little for himself. There has always been a man at his service who does pretty much everything for him, except the obvious, if you know what I mean.

Well, Mr. X, decided to go swimming one afternoon without his aide. He was probably feeling a tang rebellious and wanted to prove to the uninterested world at large that he was perfectly capable of looking after himself. You can probably also imagine the pout that he fashioned on his face as he strutted off to the pool.

In all likelihood, he had had a minor row with the poor assistant who, probably was smiling quietly to himself, knowing intimately what his lord and master was capable or not capable of.

Mintu was greeted with a cheery "Good Afternoon" by Mr. X, who had been indoctrinated with all the niceties of social manners and etiquette by the Anglo-Indian teachers who had tutored him. Like Mr. X, there were others who had migrated to the pool to temper the soaring temperatures. So far, so good. Mr. X changed into his swimming gear with remarkable agility, balancing himself, on one foot and then the next. After this nimble and gymnastic performance, he had his shower and went in for his dip.

As with the laws of buoyancy, he had no difficulty in floating around for forty-five minutes. He exchanged polite conversation with his fellow swimmers, and then bounced out of the water and went to the changing room. He took another quick shower, and picked up the boxers. What followed remains etched in my visual, mental, and auditory sensibilities.

A fellow swimmer, who was also done with cooling down in the pool, came into the changing room and scanned the place for his boxers. Fairly soon, he spotted them moulded to the generous anatomy of Mr. X, relaxing on a chair. Irritation, amazement, and finally disbelief contorted his visage before he blurted out, "Mr. X, you have worn my boxers?"

The man in question looked mildly apologetic, a little sheepish, and then turned for help, expecting his aide. He had had enough physical exertion for the day.

"Oh, of course. Today he was on his own." Realisation dawned. Pulling himself up straight, he instructed the flabbergasted Mintu, "Take these off and hand them over to the gentleman. He needs to wear them. He cannot go home without his boxers, can he? Find my boxers and put them on me."

It is important to point out here that the two pairs of boxers had precious little in common in terms of colour or design, but one could not blame poor Mr. X. After all, he was not used to managing his own affairs.

"But Sir, but Sir," mumbled the confused and distraught Mintu, trying his level best to be helpful, but also trying to hold on to his own dignity and self-respect at the same time. "I will just give you your boxers. The rules here prohibit me from helping you change. I am giving you a chair in the changing room, for you to sit and do the needful comfortably." Unable to find any argument to counter Mintu, Mr. X went off to the changing room and came out in a little while, in his own boxers, and handed over the ones he had been wearing to the rightful owner, who by then was speechless.

Needless to say, Mr. X never tried to exercise his show of independence again.

As I mentioned, I had no idea swimming could be so entertaining. Mr. Z was fond of his afternoon martini. After retirement the afternoons stretched into the balmy evenings and the partiality to the drink stretched too. That particular day, the stretch had been to a snapping point. The table had had many visitors through the hours but Mr. Z had been the constant occupant of the chair through all the conversations. He then decided to clear his fuzzy head with an energising swim. As usual, our man Mintu was on duty. The senior citizen trundled into the changing room, and swayed out in his swimming trunks and sauntered off to the pool.

After a couple of leisurely laps, he paddled off to the side for a break and to inspect the happenings around him. The swim had refreshed his body but not his mind. He looked around, as if surveying his own little fiefdom. There was a lady in the pool, immersed in her routine exercise. She interested him. And as he watched her more, his interest grew. Soon, he was swimming alongside her. The lady, uncomfortable with the distance between them, moved away. "You swim like a swan and I have been watching you. I feel like doing a duet dance with you, as we swim. I know that you were a member of the water ballet team and so was I. How about a two member ballet performance?" he slurred.

Alarmed, the lady swam strongly to the ladder, with Mr. Z in pursuit. "Don't disappoint me. Rarely do we have the pool to ourselves to dance away our cares." In a raised voice the lady answered, "I have no desire to dance with you and I have no cares to share with you. Behave yourself, otherwise I will raise an alarm."

The ever vigilant Mintu had heard the agitated tone and he rushed to the pool. By then the lady had reached the ladder and she hastily went off, giving Mr. Z a killing look. Mintu's arrival checked the raging hormones in Mr. Z and he dipped his tipsy head in the cool chlorine water. Matter managed, Mintu quietly waited for Mr. Z to step out of the pool and beat a retreat to the changing room.

After a while he found a contrite Mr. Z sitting on a chair, with puffy eyes. "I have made a fool of myself. Old age is tough, Mintu. I miss the energy, confidence and the zest of youth. In my prime, I could have enjoyed my drinks, charmed the ladies and not appeared like I was crossing any boundary. I have lost that touch or perhaps that touch does not sit well with an old man. I thank you in advance for not discussing this incident with anyone."

There was yet another occurrence that comes to mind as I write about my 'swimming adventures'. Mr. Y is an absent-minded brilliant individual who periodically wanders off into his own world. When such bouts happen in public view, things can occasionally get a bit awkward.

It was a hot afternoon, as is most natural in a tropical country in June. Mintu, as usual, poor soul, was on duty in the changing room. He had had a rather long day, and the sweltering heat had sapped his chirpy energy. In the quiet humidity of the changing room, his eyelids grew heavy and droopy. At one moment, he compelled his eyes to open, and what he saw had him scampering at a speed that would put a cheetah to shame.

Mr. Y had shed his clothes, and in his bout of absentmindedness had ambled out of the changing room. He was determinedly making his way to the swimming pool!

Mintu's shocked, "Sir, Sir" rang out across the corridor and the enclosed area of the pool. Looking faintly curious,

Mr. Y turned around and stared enquiringly at Mintu, who by now had managed to reach his target with a towel. Hastily wrapping it around Mr. Y, he guided him back to the safety of the changing room.

A social disaster had just been averted in the nick of time! Mintu, as you can well imagine, is a storehouse of rather delicate anecdotes.

8

The Fruitseller

Puja was exhausted. All of thirty-two, she had carried the family chores on her frail shoulders for the past eleven years. An ailing father-in-law, the only one who was genuinely fond of her in her husband's home, a demanding mother-in-law, sisters-in-law who were perpetually on extended holiday at their parents' home even after marriage, her own young children and a busy husband were hers to look after. Her older brother-in-law, Vikrant and his wife Nisha lived in another city.

It was the *Satya-Narayan puja* once again. All the arrangements needed to be completed. Cleaning of the room, cutting of the fruits and putting the items together for the *prasad*[1]. The priest was expected in the evening and her mother-in-law, Nimmi was charged, as usual. She had invited her friends, neighbours and relatives for the event and barked orders at the servants. "Don't think you are doing me a favour. All this is for your own good. Working for the *puja* will earn you points to stack into your account for your next birth. You will be born into a more prosperous family and have servants working for you."

It was late afternoon when she walked into the *puja* room for a final survey and came out thunder-faced.

---

[1] Food served to the deity and then distributed in His or Her name to the devotees.

"Puja," she shouted hysterically. "Do you not want the purest blessings for the family? After all these years how could you…?" She was almost apoplectic.

Puja stood, rooted, bewildered. "What is it, Ma?" she asked, softly.

"Have you seen the bananas meant for the *shinni*[2]? It is the wrong variety and unfit for a holy occasion. I will not allow it to be used and mar my *puja*."

"Ali probably did not have the other variety."

"Who? Did you say Ali sold the fruits? Are you out of your mind? Go immediately and buy the appropriate fruits. Don't breathe a word of this to anyone. I will sprinkle Ganges water and purify the entire room. I cannot understand where your brain is."

Puja dragged herself to the market seething inside, to buy the 'correct' banana for the pleasure of the gods and to pacify her mother-in-law. While the guests were socialising after the ceremony, she went to her father-in-law with the *prasad*. He was waiting to speak to her after listening to his wife's tirade. "Puja, I am not blind to what is happening in the house. I will not be there for long to protect you. She is my wife but I cannot take responsibility for her thoughts and actions. Just as you need to take responsibility for protecting yourself. You need to speak up. You have my support."

Feeling much calmer and empowered, Puja prepared herself. She imagined the response that she would have

---

[2] An offering made at Satya-Narayan Puja as per Hindu customs. Shinni is made with flour, bananas, sugar, milk, nuts, etc.

loved to give in various situations, but had held back. Afraid of raised voices and harsh confrontations, she had been giving in. The imaginary replay, with her clearly voicing her thoughts and feelings, gave her relief and confidence. She practised in her free moments.

A few days later, four adults sat down for breakfast while the children were at school. "Nisha called me this morning," said Puja. "Vikrant and she have had a major row over his drinking habit. They had gone for a party and he misbehaved there. She wants him to join a rehab centre. Besides, he has another issue as we all know, though he says that he has put it behind him. Nisha has proof that he has not. She is planning on staying with her parents for a while to think things over. She is not convinced that there is any point in putting any more time and energy into the marriage."

"Of course, the easiest option is to blame my son for all their problems. He never had these complications before marriage. His wife has driven him to this with her constant demands."

Puja felt anger surging through her. "Ma, when your daughters stay here because of their marital issues, I have never heard you say that they have any role to play there. It is always the fault of the in-laws or their husbands. Nisha is also the daughter of some family."

"How dare you speak to me like this? Your parents have not taught you to respect elders?"

"My parents have taught me to speak up for what is right and what I believe in. Unfortunately, I had forgotten my lessons. And I will not have anyone talking badly of my parents in their absence when they cannot speak up for themselves."

"First, you sully the purity of my *puja* and now you are answering back. My husband and son will not put up with this."

"I am merely stating my views. If the two men think I am wrong, let them speak to me. Besides, all this talk of sullying your *puja* seems very weak. We all know that your son Vikrant has a Muslim girlfriend. He spends hours with her. They even go off on holidays together. Does he get sullied?"

Puja had spoken quietly but firmly, without any fear creeping into her voice or body language. She looked at the two men straight in the eye, willing them to speak.

Her husband, who had always shied away from any altercation with his mother, especially when it concerned his wife, could not hide behind any excuse now. Watching his wife's new stance stoked in him a grudging respect. "I agree with Puja. Whatever logic she has given makes complete sense. There is no point in dragging this matter. If Nisha decides to go away she has every reason to. She needs to live her life her way."

Her father-in-law, true to his promise, added, "I am happy that you have explained your point clearly and logically, Puja. Complicating one's life with all these rigid notions is so counter-productive. I have never mentioned this to your mother-in-law but when I visited the market to buy fruits and vegetables, Karim would always keep a packet ready for me with the choicest fruits. I remember him telling me, *'Aaap ke liye khas phal rakha hai. Puja ke liye bilkul sahi hai.'* (I have kept these fruits especially for you. They are right for your *puja*.) It was a matter of pride for him to give me the best fruits for the occasion. The fact that he was a Muslim made no difference. He respected my requirement and I was grateful to him for that. The other option would be to own my own farm or orchard if I got into all these traps!"

"This is like a conspiracy against me planned by the three of you. I have dedicated my entire life to looking after your welfare, warding off any harm through my prayers and what I believe to be sacrosanct methods of worship to keep the gods happy so that they bless and protect you and this is what I get. It is a combined attack to prove me wrong and make all my actions look ridiculous. This is humiliating me." The mother-in-law played the victim card.

"That has not been our intention at all, Nimmi. Our wish is to free you from your own self-created cage that cramps you. It is a matter of great joy if someone from a different religion helps you in your worship to offer the best to your beloved gods. Why create problems?

We have been married for nearly forty years and I truly appreciate your dedication to me and your caring for me. Have you forgotten the time when little Vikrant was very unwell and it was our peon Zakir who went to the mosque to pray for him and gave you something that he believed would help him? I remember you putting it away carefully."

"That was a personal relationship of love and affection. But these are societal beliefs. How can I break free of them? We live in a society where we need to follow these practices," replied Nimmi.

"Just listen to yourself speak. You are trying to justify your own views to yourself. Relationships are between humans and they are personal. We enjoyed the food that Zakir would share with us during his festivals and you would always keep aside for his family whatever special was cooked during ours. And that made you so happy. Why not just go with what comes naturally and makes you feel easy and good?"

Puja walked across to her mother-in-law and held her close. The older lady sat stiffly for a while and then crumpled into tears. "All these years I have been struggling to do what I thought was socially acceptable when it would have been so much easier to not bother... and that is going against me today..."

Sixty-five-year-old Nimmi got up. "I need some air. I am going for a walk." Saying this she left the discomfiture of the heated conversation and went to the park. And sitting on the bench gave herself permission to weep.

Over forty years ago, Nimmi was known in her college for her blithe spirit. Heedless of any societal fetters, she had chosen her beau. Classmates, the two were inseparable. Yet... Feeling the tightness in her chest, Nimmi whispered hoarsely, "Why, why could you not fight for us? What made you so weak and fearful? I was willing to take on my family, challenge all their misgivings because I was so sure of us, our love and commitment to each other. My mother had threatened to never see my face again and even that I was prepared to accept."

Questions she had buried deep inside, welled over. There had never been a closure. But there had been a violent reaction. He happened to be a Muslim. Unlike her, he had given in to family pressure. They were not willing to accept this union. Too ashamed to tell her in person, he had informed her of his decision through words on paper.

Shaken and shocked, Nimmi turned to stone. She told herself she would not give him the privilege of her tears. And the carefree and buoyant Nimmi gradually turned to one entangled in the quagmire of societal prejudices, a stranger even to herself.

Feeling lighter after releasing her hurt, pain and anger, she sought her lost happy spirit. "I cannot do this to my family and myself. I don't even like myself as I have become in my bitter reactionary mode. I must let go."

Slowly, she made her way back home. Her husband was waiting for her. He took in her swollen eyes and going close, held her hands. "I am there, your centre, even when you are estranged from yourself. I will not let you down, even if I disagree with you."

Something in his tone made Nimmi look at him questioningly. They had never talked about her past. She held his gaze as he nodded with an understanding smile and spoke, "I've known all along. One experience cannot make you distrust everyone and colour your views. That is not who you are, Nimmi."

There was silence as Nimmi held his hands tightly. "Thank you. Thank you so much for always being there and accepting me with all the complexities. And for helping me get in touch with myself again."

9

Invincible

Roddur Sen. For those uninitiated in the Bengali language, *'roddur'* means sunshine.

His name irked him. It hadn't initially, but as he grew older it seemed to provoke and taunt him, highlighting his inadequacies, reminding him that to deserve this name he had to live it. "You have me as your name. I symbolise light, heat, energy, power. I blaze my own trail. I am under no one's command. I breathe life. I can scorch and heal. I am invincible. You have to live up to me."

And so Roddur learnt to challenge, stretch and push himself to shine up to his name.

He remembered an incident in Class Two. When school got over he saw his mother from a distance, waiting along with other mothers, to take the children home. His little hands flew up in an eager wave. He had asked her to cook '*pulao* and *mangsho*[1]' for him, and had been thinking of the sumptuous lunch that was waiting for him. His excitement energised his baby legs into a run, and his face broke into a happy smile. As he came to her, she took his bag and asked, "So, how much did you get?"

"In what?" asked a bewildered seven-year-old Roddur.

---

[1] Flavoured rice (pilaf) and mutton.

"In your maths exam, of course. Your classmates have got back their papers. Romit has got full marks, and his mother was showing his paper to all of us."

The smile froze. A shadow of fear darkened his eyes. Roddur had been careless, and two of his sums were wrong. He had got ten marks short of the boy with full marks. He had disappointed his mother.

His mother did not utter a word. Her body was rigid as they sat in the car and Roddur tried to snuggle up to her. She told him, "The *pulao* and meat will have to wait. It will be your prize when you learn not to be careless and ensure that you get everything right."

Roddur had rice, *dal*[2] and an uninspiring vegetable for lunch that day. His mother's disappointment had flavoured even her cooking.

He grew into a winning machine.

"You have to set your standard at the top rung of the ladder. In the past two generations in your father's family, no one has ever come second. If you break the tradition, people will laugh at us and mock us and say how sad it is that such a glorious tradition has been broken."

Roddur had believed all this. And internalised it without questioning. Years later, he wondered who had kept the record. He became a hard-nosed achiever. People admired him for his tenacity. He maintained the family tradition, and the 'prize meals' were there at home. But it never satisfied Roddur. Instead of disappointment, the family meals were now flavoured with parental pride,

---

[2] Lentils.

even a dash of arrogance, not love and acceptance of *him* with all his incompleteness.

"I wish someone would ask me what I want, what makes me happy, how I would like to spend my free time, do I want to be a loner at the top all the time with hardly any friends," he would talk to himself.

Sometimes when the effort to excel seemed overwhelming, an inner voice spoke to him, "You want to be the worthy son, don't you? This way you can be sure that they will love you with all their heart." There was always a price for love.

Roddur grew to become the CEO of his own pharmaceutical company. He immersed himself in ground-breaking research and developed medicines for restricting cancerous growths. The company was world renowned. He 'won' the girl he wanted, and they had a boy, Gaurav.

But Roddur never insisted that Gaurav come first in class, to maintain the family tradition.

His parents were old now. They were in their seventies and lived with him. While travelling back from one of his business trips, Roddur had a severe pain in his head and fell unconscious. It was a chartered flight. He was rushed to a top-of-the-line hospital. MRIs and scans revealed that he had a brain tumour, malignant and aggressive. The scope for treatment was limited. He had only a few months to live.

Roddur did not want any invasive surgery. He knew the condition only too well, and wanted to spend his last days in peace, at home.

As his mother sat next to him, stroking his head, her face ashen, he said, "Ma, you never taught me how to lose. This is a battle I cannot win, but I hope that won't stop you from giving me '*pulao* with *mangsho*'."

Years later, I found this story amongst my father's papers. He had written it when he was bedridden, in the last couple of weeks before he left us. I knew there was a background to his being so obsessed with his work. I now understood what it was. Circumstances had put him on the roller coaster, and he did not know how to get off, until fate decided for him.

To me he was a father I would trade with none other. In school I was the son of the legendary ex-student, Roddur Sen. The headmaster in my time, had been a senior teacher in my father's school days. I never topped my class and neither was I a music prodigy. If anything, I was a huge disappointment to the teaching faculty. I bunked classes, never missed an opportunity to let off steam on the huge school grounds, playing some game or the other, copied assignments from my nerdy friends and did not hesitate to ask for their help during exams.

"You must have inherited your father's genes in some field? Why is it invisible, Gaurav? We had such hopes and expectations. Don't you have any responsibility?" my House Master Mr. Rajan asked.

Tired of constantly being compared to my father and told that I was no good, I retorted cheekily, "Sir, I am a late bloomer. I will explode into prominence when the time is right and I have found my niche. I will inform you myself." I was in class eleven and convinced that

I could take on the world. Of course, I could not and my father was summoned.

"What have you done this time?" my father whispered, when we were sitting together.

The one understanding we had was that I would never lie to him. "You will be my son, regardless of what you do and I know that you will never do anything really terrible that you need to hide. I have faith in your boundaries." I understand today that this was a loaded comment. I felt accepted as I was but at the same time I was very aware there were clear limits even to my mischief. My father had taught me accountability for my actions.

"Mr. Rajan wondered why I had not inherited any of your genes and I gave an answer he did not like."

My father smiled.

In the headmaster's office, a huge wooden desk sat between him and us. As we sat down, I remember the feel of my father's fingers curled around mine, under the table, unseen by the headmaster. "Whatever it is, we will face it together," was his calm assurance. We were a team.

After our class twelve exams I went out with my friends and got drunk. It was the first time this had happened. I got back very late. My father was asleep. I remember waking him up and telling him that we needed to talk. "Okay. I am listening," he said.

"We went to Ajay's house this evening and had drinks. I had more than I should have and got drunk. Then we walked on the streets and created a noise, singing and dancing, disturbing the neighbours and they complained to the guard who threatened to take us to the police station if we did not go back home immediately. So here I am."

Even when he heard this, my father did not lose his sense of humour. After I finished blurting out my misdoings, he looked at me and said, "I'm glad you informed me. Tomorrow morning if someone calls me, to tell me what my son has done, I can tell him that I already know, because my son himself has told me. And if God contacts me to give some more details, I can tell him, "'Wait, I need to check with my son to know what the facts are.'"

It was his faith in me and his loving acceptance of all my shortcomings that kept me on track.

As it happened, the Roddur genes did manifest themselves, but in a different avatar. I was always interested in studying the human mind and went on to become a psychiatrist of repute.

And I did keep my word to Mr. Rajan. During one of my visits to my alma mater, I made it a point to meet and tell him, "Sir, I have kept my promise and have come to inform you myself. My book on psychiatry is being used across the world."

He laughed and said, "Gaurav, you are a chip off the old block. And your father will be proud of you, wherever he is."

10

No Less A Son

Nathan scrutinised himself from all angles. The full length Belgian mirror was brutally honest. At twenty-three, he drew furtive glances from the girls at any gathering. His antennae alerted him to the excited whispers that whizzed by him when he stepped into the room, invariably clad in long *kurtas, churidar* and a casual scarf. 'Smart Casual'. The description suited him perfectly.

The obsessive trait in Nathan was piqued by his image. The cheekbones were not quite as etched as he would have liked, the abs not completely washboard. "No more indulgences," he rebuked his reflection.

Then came the reply. "Stop this blame game. You have a problem, you sort it out. The hungry look is your fetish, not mine, and neither do I want to replicate an ironing board. You are insecure. Just admit it."

Chastised, Nathan glared at the image defiantly. The eyes met in a cold duel.

There was a loud, sharp knock on the door and Nathan snapped out of his reverie. "Why do you have to be so damned aggressive? What is it you want?" he asked. He was sure it was his younger brother.

"Just checking to see whether you are asleep or awake or in some other world. Devisha has come with her parents. She wants to talk to you."

Nathan felt his muscles contract. Taking a deep breath he answered, "I'll be there in a minute."

She was the epitome of classical beauty. The expressive kohl-lined eyes and her taut and languid appeal had driven many young men to sleeplessness. A student of English, she was articulate, of unquestionable lineage and all her vibes clearly indicated that she was his for taking. And yet....

He struggled. The voice inside was loud. And repetitive. "You are a weirdo and incapable of normal human emotions. You don't deserve this adulation. Go live in that shadowy world. I am ashamed to be associated with you."

Nathan would get up, drink cold water, and feel it trickle down the agitated chamber of his body. Guilt, shame, anger, confusion, fear—all combined into a fierce flood of emotions.

He remembered his first date. All of sixteen, on the brink of manhood, he had taken his classmate to a movie. Sitting in the last seats, they had hardly watched the film. Elina, more experienced in the ways of the world, had made the first move and they groped each other in the darkness. She had called him a few times after that, but he had avoided any other outing. Then she gave up, much to his relief. He couldn't quite explain that feeling.

"So how was it?" his cousin had asked, and Nathan had muttered a vague response. "Already so possessive! For all your good boy looks, you are one cool operator. Give us some tips," he pressed, making Nathan uncomfortable.

He tried to hedge him off. "Trade secrets are not meant to be shared. Develop your own, original touch."

Quick came the repartee, "Touch. Ah. Now I know. You have acquired a special familiarity with 'touches'."

The years ticked by, gradually confirming to Nathan what he had instinctively understood about himself. His preferences were unlike most of his peers. He appreciated women, could be great friends with them, they confided in him and found him understanding, but he could not respond the way they desired.

"No one is good enough for him. He is waiting for Venus," his friends would say. But he knew otherwise.

There was no confidante to share his feelings with, at home or outside. His father, a hard-nosed businessman, was rigid and unforgiving. The aggressive pride in being the man of the family, the provider and decision-maker, who had sired two perfect male specimens, left no space on his canvas for any other stroke, especially one that would mar his 'maleness'. His progeny were meant to validate his masculinity.

No one knew this better than Nathan. He remembered the night when he, a seven-year-old, had tried to tell his father, man-to-man, that the family driver had been making strange advances towards him when he found Nathan alone in the car. "I don't like the way he touches me," he'd said. "He sits next to me, very close and takes my hand and puts it into his pants. I tried to pull my hand away but he threatened to leave me on the road."

His father's reaction was sharp. "I wish you would stop imagining things. The driver has been with us for the past decade, and has given us no reason for complaint. You are a boy. Behave like one."

Scared by the outburst, Nathan had never complained again, but the abuse had continued a few more years. At one point, when he tried shouting at the driver and telling him he would complain to his father, the response was a dry laugh and the words, "What will he say? I know his secrets. For all his high and mighty attitude, he is like any street-side Romeo. I know about his mistresses. Let him say something to me, and I will leak his secret."

And so little Nathan paid the price for his father's lusty escapades in the sleazy hotels of Kolkata.

Nathan's mother, a traditional homemaker, restricted herself to the chores of the household. She submitted to her husband, only because she was afraid of handling the consequences of rebellion. Her quiet presence was a balm to Nathan as he grew up, but he had never discussed his experiences with her.

Pulling himself together, Nathan walked out of his room to meet Devisha. After exchanging a few formalities she came and sat next to him. Giving him an intimate smile she said, "So good to see you. We have not met in a long while. I hope to see you at my birthday bash. You have to be there. I want you to meet all my friends."

The two families got on well, and there was an unspoken understanding that the children would marry. Nathan's father was conscious it would be a big boost for his business, since his range of contacts would increase vastly.

Devisha was only too willing, and Nathan had been trying to buy time, saying he needed to complete his Masters in Business Administration before getting into any commitment. Now even that excuse was invalid. He had just been offered a lucrative position with a well reputed firm after earning the degree.

"Hello Shamji, I have missed our *addas*[1]," said Nathan's father, addressing Devisha's father. He had just got back from work and was happy to see his friend.

"Same here", replied Shamji and added, "Actually we were hoping to meet all of you. Other than inviting you for Devisha's birthday we thought we could discuss some important matters."

"Yes, of course. I have been thinking of having a conversation with you too."

"Now that Nathan has completed his MBA and has been offered such a coveted job, we were hoping we could finalise the wedding date. Both of them are at a marriageable age and it is always good to do the right thing at the right age, don't you agree?"

"I couldn't agree more. This matter has been on my mind. Children nowadays have such a fear of marriage, but once they tie the knot everything works out. Look at us, we didn't have any choice but things have worked out fine."

"We simply did as we were told by our parents and lived with it. Too many choices today, and too much of exposure really causes confusion and you look for

---

[1] Get togethers.

problems where there aren't any. Besides, I'm sure you too would like to become grandparents when you are mobile enough to really enjoy the grandchildren."

"You have spoken my deepest wish," said Nathan's father. "Nothing would make us happier and where else would we get such a beautiful and accomplished daughter-in-law? We will call the priest, and..."

Before he could complete, Nathan said, "At least you can ask me before committing on my behalf. I have nothing against Devisha. I admire her and value her friendship but am extremely sorry, I cannot get married. Please don't make this whole thing so difficult. Do try and understand."

There was stunned silence, as if the very breath had been sucked out of those present. The tension was palpable. Expressions ranged from disbelief, hurt and anguish to raw anger. Then his father spoke. "Understand what? That my son is a wimp?"

Nathan felt claustrophobic, as if he was being pulled into a tunnel. He refused to enter a public slinging match with his father and instead addressed Devisha and asked for her forgiveness. He then walked away from the gathering, entered his room, sat with his head in his hands and wept.

Struggling to accept himself, he felt a further disgrace at not being able to be a 'son' to his parents.

A familiar fragrance wafted in. He heard the door shut softly and saw the blurred image of his mother standing next to him. She held him close and said, "You have nothing to worry about or feel ashamed of. You are no less a man than any other male, and you are no less a son to me than you have always been."

"You understood?" whispered Nathan.

She nodded and held him tight. Both had tears drenching their cheeks—his of relief, for being loved unconditionally and accepted just as he was and hers of love, understanding and empathy.

The wheel turned for him. Serotonin surged inside and Nathan felt armoured. He felt liquid confidence rush through his veins when he turned to his mother and said, "Amma, I have asked for a posting to Mumbai. The package includes accommodation and the company has its own designated apartments. I would love it if you come and stay with me. It will be your home and you will have all the freedom to do what you want."

His mother looked happily startled and then a shadow crossed her face. "What will your father do? How will he manage? For twenty-five years I have looked after him, meeting all his requirements."

"And, who has looked after your needs? I have not been blind to what has been happening. I know you were a good student. It is you who taught me. I also heard from your father that you had wanted to become a professor. But you were not allowed to study further after marriage though you had been promised that. Tell me what you want, what will make you happy?"

Their conversation was cut short by the door being kicked open and his father stood there, breathing fire. "How dare you insult me? You are not fit to be my son. I have a reputation in society as a respected and successful man and you have rubbed it to the ground.

I have provided you everything that you needed and you have just brought me shame."

Two things happened, almost simultaneously. Nathan felt violated and enraged. The fear to react dissipated and he was ready for combat. His mother's assurance had helped build his courage.

"Yes, you sired me and that has been your only 'glorious' contribution in my life. Other than that, it is you who has been a complete failure as a father. The very basic thing a child needs is protection and you failed miserably. What my preferences are today also has a lot to do with you. I have accepted myself, but can you?

When I told you about the driver, you refused to do anything. He was continuously abusing me and I went to you for help. I felt defenceless, helpless and at his mercy. What did you do, as my father, guardian and protector? You snapped at me and discarded it as my imagination and asked me to behave myself. You did not believe me. How do you think it made me feel? Totally abandoned, alone and vulnerable, dismissed by the one person whom I looked up to and trusted. I had felt so sure you would be by my side and take care of my troubles.

Instead, you continued to keep him in your pay because you had secrets that he knew. I am not afraid of you anymore. I am well aware of your so called reputation and respect. The same driver called you a road-side Romeo. He knew that he was immune from any action because he was the accomplice to your debauchery. At least I am honest about who I am. You lied to your wife, to me and my brother. You don't need me to rub your reputation to the ground. You have done it very successfully by yourself."

His father was beside himself with rage. He could not believe his ears and not having words to defend himself with, raised his hands to hit Nathan, saying, "You are insulting your mother and me. You are an utter disgrace and are using allegations to cover up for your ineptitude. Your mother and I will have nothing more to do with you."

Before he could touch Nathan, it was Nathan's mother who gripped her husband's hands and gave him a resounding slap across his face.

"I have known for a long time about your lusty escapades and filthy lies. I chose to ignore them and put up with you because I thought I had no choice but to stay here and be with the children. They would have been lost. It appears they were lost despite my making the difficult choice. My effort seems to have been in vain. I had no idea that Nathan had been abused so brutally and you did nothing about it, in spite of him telling you. For that there is no forgiveness. I will have everything to do with my children as I always have and I love them as they are. After this, it is not possible for me to live with you."

It seemed as if a bolt of lightning had struck the father. The slap on the face appeared to punch the wind out of him. He stood there, deflated. The man who was always so puffed up about himself, stood there, naked, in the exposure of his vulnerabilities and weaknesses.

Few weeks later, Nathan left for Mumbai with his mother, with promises of a happier and more fulfilling life, where each person could live and grow as they were meant to. He was not just "no less a son to his mother". His brother was studying in Delhi. The recent events had awakened in him a new-found respect for his elder brother.

11

Bewitching Sundarban

Sitting on the boat with the cool water breeze blowing through your hair and gliding along the river with the breathing roots of the mangrove forest, the Sundarban, on either side, on the world's largest tidal delta, is soporific. And if you are on the boat long enough you can experience the tidal play. High tide or *jwar* has the water flooding the forest, with just the tops of the trees bobbing on the water table. Then, as if set on a timer, the receding water with the *bhata*[1] leaves the trees balanced on stilts, the exposed roots. It is pure magic with the moon's energy and the water expanse engaged in a cosmic dance enacted on Earth.

And as the boat eases into the little creek flanked by the dense verdant forest on both sides, the voice of the forest guide cuts into my Nature induced trance. "Don't let your alertness get lulled into sleep by this beauty. We who live here love our home, the open wilderness and the freedom of the wind but are aware of the jaws of death even in our dreams—the saw in the crocodile's snout and the mighty canines of the Royal Bengal tiger as also the venom of the King Cobra. It is a daily battle of wits, presence of mind, strength of nerves and cunning, between man and beast."

---

1 Low tide.

I could see he was very serious about warning me in case I dipped my hand in the water to simply feel the flow and the temperature. "The tiger on land and the crocodile in water—they don't give you much of an option other than to stay on the boat. Yet, there are those who go deep into the forest to collect honey and others who risk going into the narrow creeks to catch crabs and fish in their small row boats. They really live life on the edge to make a living."

His voice had dropped low as he said these words. The tone was grave. I could sense that he had lived the warning.

"It seems like you have had a close encounter."

"Oh yes. Not once but a few times. So, believe me, I am talking from experience. Sometimes I get nightmares even now though it happened years ago. In these tranquil and balmy surroundings when you are face to face with danger in its extreme form, is when you realise just how minuscule your power is in comparison to Nature's raw and untamed instinct and brute energy."

"Could you share some encounters with us?"

"Hmm...I don't want to frighten you but at the same time it is good to know the reality. It was low tide and my parents were on the river bank, throwing the fishing net into the water to get some fish for our meal. Our staple diet is fish and rice. I was a ten year old standing a little away from them, curious about what fish we would get to eat. To be able to throw the net a bit further, my father stepped into the water and his feet hit something hard. In a flash he was pulled into the river and felt the jaws of death crunching into his leg. For us, who live in a warrior mode with the death threat looming large all around us, our instinct and reflexes work at supersonic speed.

My mother immediately threw the net around my father and started pulling him towards herself with all her might, screaming out for help. I held on to her waist and desperately gave her support. Villagers who were around and those who heard her, rushed and it became a tug of war between the mighty predator of the water and the human team on land. The strength of one crocodile is difficult to even imagine. As it heaved its prey deeper into the river, we, a human chain, dug our feet into the clay and pulled in the opposite direction. After what seemed like eternity, the grip of the jaws slackened and we could yank my bleeding and semi-conscious father out of the water. He was taken by boat to the hospital in the town close by and it took him months to recover. His leg was permanently damaged but he lived to tell his tale."

We, the tourists on the boat, had practically stopped breathing as the story unfolded. It took us a breath or two after the story got over, to respond.

"Thank God for your mother's immediate reaction. He is safe, alive and you are telling us your unbelievable tale. This will become a part of the folklore of your village. What an experience!"

"Today, I can joke a little about it and say that it was not too happy a crocodile that swam away. My parents couldn't stop trembling for a long time—the combination of dread, fear and relief was a peculiar concoction."

"And what about you? How were you feeling?"

"To be honest, I was numb for a long time. My parents wrapped me up and then held me tight. They were weeping tears of relief. It was when my mother and I went home, after admitting father in the hospital, and recounted what had happened, that the enormity of the incident slowly sunk in and I needed to be with someone all the time. The trauma has never really gone away."

We were all quiet for a while, absorbing the experience vicariously, ensuring that our fingers and toes were well within the confines of the boat, fearfully eyeing the calm water for evidence of any scaly, teethy creature stealthily swimming next to us, biding its time for luck to turn in its favour.

It was a sobering thought to say the least, for even the most adventurous and dare devil amongst us. We were ambling along mid river, squinting to spot a deer, a wild boar, rare birds or if the forest goddess, Bonbibi, granted us a boon, perhaps the lord of the jungle himself—the elusive Royal Bengal tiger.

The voice of the guide sliced through our unidimensional focus.

We continued our conversation.

"It is very possible that you cannot spot him but he is watching you from the shadows through the dense network of leaves in the forest as the rays of the sun play peek-a-boo using the green lattice. This is his land, his kingdom and his roar makes every creature shake like a flimsy wisp of hair in the breeze."

"That is quite a creepy thought actually. Almost feels like we are being stalked. But then we are in his territory and he has every reason to be suspicious, especially when there are so many among us who refuse to respect the jungle laws."

"Yes, you have hit a very sensitive nerve. The loud music and raucous noise on many boats is even more jarring in the stillness and incorruptible silence of the pristine forest. Sometimes I find my own breathing too loud when we are in the core area. The animals get very disturbed."

"Have you ever stepped into the jungle to collect honey?"

"Yes, I have. We went in a group and a few amongst us were seasoned honey gatherers, though accidents happen with even the most experienced. I can tell you another account of a few of my friends who were initially poachers in this forest but have now joined various organisations as fierce protectors of the jungle."

We were all ears. His riveting narrative about his crocodile meeting had whetted our appetite.

"This happened a few years ago. We were on a boat, a medium-sized one, with about half a dozen tourists. The crew consisted of four of us, all well versed with life in the Sundarban. There were two open areas on both ends of the boat with the driver space in the centre. The small kitchen area was downstairs and the cook had served tea and snacks in the open area. It was a relaxed holiday ambience and the guests were chitchatting over mugs of Darjeeling tea, munching *pakoras*[2], enjoying the

---

[2] Vegetable fritters.

tranquillity of the water, jungle and the cool autumn breeze. No pressure, no deadline, no urgency.

I was occasionally pointing out a bird on a tree, a water monitor on the bank and giving details about the local vegetation and the forest itself. My eyes scanned the surroundings and then I happened to look up at the roof of the boat just above the place where the guests had gathered. It was yet another frozen-in-time moment for me. To be more specific, it was a 'frozen me' instant for me. I was looking at a full grown king cobra coiled around the top of the pole that supported the roof. Any moment it could decide to investigate the boat and unravel itself to slide down."

Needless to say, all of us on the boat immediately peered with pinched eyes for any hint of a tail or darting forked tongue suspended in any hidden corner of the canopy above us. The guide, in some manner, enjoying the ruffling impact of his tale, smiled and assured us not to worry since the boat had been carefully sanitised, a term used in common parlance now.

We breathed a trifle shakily and urged him to continue.

"So as you can visualise, the situation was tense to say the least. I could not tell the guests because they would panic and we could not have our tourists hurtling around the boat. There was the question of balance and safety and we could not agitate the reptile in any way. We were in the middle of the river. Anyone falling over out of sheer desperation would mean the crocodile's jaws and the river bank for stepping out would invite the teeth of the striped jungle king. I had to keep my cool, be very calm and plan on a course of action. I needed to consult with the other crew members without in any way making the guests unnecessarily curious.

Gathering all my latent acting skills, a while later I told my guests that they needed to step on to the other side of the boat since the cook would be setting out lunch for us and needed free space. They fortunately agreed without any hint of suspicion and I went off for a word with my friends.

As I mentioned, my friends, the rest of the hands on the boat, had initially been poachers and were very skilled with their aim and creating tools, knew how to think on their feet and above all could keep their calm in extremely dangerous situations. Quickly summing up the spot we were in, they found two long poles, the top ends of which were crossed and tied very securely to form a kind of an open noose. With just their eyes they had to decide on the girth of the cobra's neck and accordingly make the noose.

A king cobra as we all know is venomous, long, can strike from a distance and raise itself high. We wanted to save the snake and also keep everyone safe. The driver had gradually taken the boat nearer to the bank. I had walked to where the guests were to keep them engaged. Two of the most skilled crew members worked together in perfectly choreographed steps. There was absolutely no scope for any error. The timing had to be perfect. One of them struck the open end of the pole noose in one swift movement to immobilise the head of the snake. As it immediately uncoiled itself, the other person caught the tail. The timing was synchronised faultlessly. As one held the tail, the other released the head and instantly the man holding the tail swung it around and threw the snake far on to the bank of the river.

It took both the humans and the reptile some time to recover. The two men drank water and took long deep breaths with the sheer relief of averting an impending crisis and the snake gathered itself and slithered into the jungle."

We were experiencing the world through a whole new perspective. One that was entirely alien to us and yet existed not in some far off forgotten land but very close to the metropolis of Kolkata. It was beautiful, unpredictable, apparently serene and timid yet alluringly savage and wild. Enticingly threatening in its many moods and avatars.

We were informed that being caught in an unexpected storm while in the boat could be an unforgettable experience and we could understand why it would be so. Not one I would like to undergo to include in my memoirs.

We were now heading back to our resort, an ecologically sensitively planned holiday spot in a village. The thatched roofs of our cottages with mud finished walls had all the necessary amenities inside, with solar powered lighting. The little dining gazebo at a distance with bamboo furniture made for a rustic feel and blended into the green surroundings. A little pond with a charming little bridge over it was ideal to stand on and watch the fish frolicking.

The dense forest was behind us and we were drifting along the placid water, sipping on earthen cups with steaming coffee, nibbling small *nimki*[3] and watching the sun slip away into the shimmering water at the horizon, flaming the sky orange, pink, red and ochre. When we had set out in the morning on our day cruise, the tide was low and then it came in strong and the trees got submerged. We now noticed the ebb of the tide and we were still a fair distance from our destination.

The crew appeared to be conferring amongst themselves and then we were informed that it would be a while before we got back because the water level was getting too low for the boat to float. A disappearing river!

Sure enough in what appeared to be just some minutes we realised that we were or rather the boat was sitting on what appeared to be just the moist river bed. People from another boat close to ours actually stepped out of the boat and toddled off on an evening walk, picking up pebbles and larger stones. It was remarkable.

The evening deepened and on the bank next to us we saw the silhouette of a partially dry tree, its outstretched branches looking gaunt against the evening sky that nestled the setting sun on one side and the rising moon on the other. We simply gazed in awe, like a baby seeing the wondrous world for the very first time.

In its time the tide came in, the water rose and we were off. Like waiting for the barrier to be raised on a railway crossing till the train blazed by, we were given

---

[3] A deep-fried crunchy savoury snack made with seasoned flour.

the green, well bluish grey signal by Nature, releasing its sluice gates.

Back at the resort we had our evening entertainment lined up—a *jatra*[4] on a story about Bonbibi.

Dukhe, a young boy who lived with his mother was taken by his uncle to the forest to collect honey. She asked her son to call out to the forest goddess in case he was in trouble and needed protection. The team searched high and low but could not locate the golden pot, the beehives with the treasured honey.

The threat of the expedition being an absolute waste and a huge loss loomed large. The forest demon, Dakhinrai (who took the form of a tiger) appeared and struck a deal with the uncle.

Dakhinrai wanted the boy and he promised not to attack the other members of the crew and help them find the treasure. The honey was found, lots of it, and the tiger came for its prey. The boy remembered his mother's advice and called out to Bonbibi who came to his rescue. Set to music and dance with local instruments being used, the theatre won all our hearts. The entertainment did not stop there and the night was long. One of the resort managers sat with us as we enjoyed our dinner. We got talking.

"You must have had your share of close encounters with the fauna of the Sundarban. Is there any one in particular that you would like to share with us?"

---

[4] Local theatre.

"There are so many. Let me think. I could tell you about an incident that happened not long ago in this very village."

We leant forward, alert and eager to know more.

"You do know that tigers in the Sundarban swim across the river from the jungle to the villages. If there is a shortage of food or water, injury or old age, when a tiger finds it difficult to hunt in the wild it crosses over in search of cattle or goats as easy prey. Sometimes it also attacks humans.

There are large paddy fields in our village and this incident happened when the crop was ready for harvesting and the plants had grown high. It was morning and the farmers were busy tending to their crop when we heard a terrified shriek. 'Mama, mama!' A farmer screamed and ran wildly towards the huts. The others followed, raising an alarm. A huge tiger had been spotted, crouching in the midst of the tall swaying blades of paddy.

Locally the tiger is referred to as 'mama' or uncle. People rushed out, banging tins to frighten the animal away towards the river, hoping that it would swim back home. The poor confused creature did just the opposite and charged towards the village, growling and roaring, baring its teeth in a grimace.

The forest officials were informed and during the wait for their arrival there was a tsunami of fear, excitement, tension and curiosity that swept through the village. All regular work came to a complete halt with every member, grandchild to grandparent, immersed in this village shaking event. Finally, the officials arrived armed with tranquiliser injections. It requires enormous skill and patience to close in on an angry, frightened wild animal on the loose, desperately trying to find a safe shelter.

A huge crowd of excited people shouting conflicting instructions, made it nerve wracking to do the job. A herd of unruly humans can be much more daunting than a herd of wild horses on the run. The injection did find its target but not all the medicine was released. The dart was probably in a position where the tiger could pull it out with its teeth before the process could be completed.

The tiger was partially tranquillised.

This was discovered when a couple of officials went up close to inspect the animal. The medicine had had some impact and it was lying on the ground. Sensing danger in its semi-conscious state, it mustered up strength, leapt up high and let out a deafening roar. It was as if the men had been struck with a massive voltage electric current. They went flying back and one of them fell hard on the ground injuring his leg seriously.

The tiger charged away from the people, seeking sanctuary. Time in hand was short to get a hold on it to transport it to safety. The medicine was still in its system and it got tired with all the running. Another injection with the necessary dosage was administered once again and this time the medicine went in.

The drama was not yet over. Many curious villagers were insistent on getting close to the tiger and touching it. It is easy to be brave when there is no threat. It took the clever warning by a forest official that the tiger would be up any minute, to get the area cleared.

The animal was safely released into the jungle and our village was splashed all over the news channels. The villagers had a lot to talk about and of course many tall tales were manufactured too!"

It's been two days since I got back to my home of brick and mortar in Kolkata and the only disturbance I have faced is that caused by buzzing flies, high pitched musical mosquitoes and the occasional clicking of the house lizard. The 'tameness' and 'boringness' is killing me.

12
Legacy

Wearing a mustard handloom sari with a maroon border embellished with a *kalamkari*[1] blouse in the same shades, her silver locks styled into a wedge cut, Aarnavi Basu at seventy could still give a fifty-year-old lass a run for her money. In this case a race for her looks, her charm and most sprintingly the agility of her mind.

Born at a time when life for girls from 'respectable' homes normally meant a long list of 'don'ts', she had matched it with a longer list of 'do's', curated by her and her equally 'life is meant to be lived to the hilt' younger sister, Anvika.

Even for a person sitting on a tall champion race horse and looking down a classic aquiline nose, neither sister could be faulted for bad or questionable behaviour—socially, in public view. After all they were the progeny of the one and only Sikandar Basu and his wife Joline.

Rewind. Sikandar was the engine behind the generously oiled wheels of a locomotive company. 'Joyride' and 'Elan' were the luxury leisure vehicles, reminiscent of an era when socially upper crust individuals had the time and the inclination to live a life of slow breathing, watching sunrises or sunsets over numerous cups of Darjeeling tea from delicately

---

[1] Print with natural dyes.

patterned bone china tea cups or enjoying a sundowner in the balcony of a club with friends. Sikandar had managed to capture time and stop the clock in the experience offered by his 'journeys'.

His foray into the life on wheels business happened when the privilege of boredom had made him step away from his thriving jute mills that lined the banks of the Hooghly river. Money from the mills made his coffers obese. They could now be managed by his managers. The elegantly toned and timeless luxury cars gave him the class he craved for, never mind that it happened in the dusk years of his life. The sun had not yet bid adieu and the gently shaded drape of his life canvas was the ideal backdrop for all the strokes he wanted to paint.

Being on the 'must be invited' directory by the Who's Who was essential. And he made it to the invitee list for tea at the Governor's residence with his handsome wife. He took his family for a carefully planned tour of Europe, introducing them to all the nuances of art and literature. There was enough conversation material that he now had for the get-togethers with the social elite. He got himself a tutor to train him into subtleties of wine, cheese and food pairing with different drinks. Going on the Tuscany trail gave him the legitimacy to give a first-hand description of the legendary vineyards.

"It was a fascinating education of how the soil, its minerals, the temperature variations are necessary for the grapes to maintain the balance of the aroma, the acidity and the sugar. The wine tasting tours ended up with us being able to identify the fruity flavours and the minerals and the hors d'oeuvre that could accompany them."

The social glitterati were suitably impressed with his description of the various wines. "Mr. Basu, we look forward to you conducting one of the sessions in our wine club. Many of us have not had the good fortune of visiting so many vineyards and you can help fill in the gaps for us," offered a senior member of the government. Of course, Sikandar was only too happy to oblige, finding it hard to contain his excitement. He had arrived. During his discourse in the wine club, the enchantment of the Italian Riviera was thrown in for good measure. The list went on. By the time he was ready to meet his creator he had ploughed through a substantial portion of his wish bucket list.

He had instilled in his children the taste for and the appreciation of the finer things in life. Undeterred with not having a son to pass on his business and life's learning to, he poured it all into his daughters, including the intricacies of running a successful business. "Do not be intimidated by anyone trying to talk down to you about how you should lead your lives or manage the business. Be like the tigress protecting her cubs and your survival instincts will instantly come to your rescue. Remember, my genetic imprint is deep."

The sisters loved living life Queen size while keeping the legacy of the crown firmly in place. Their rich and stimulating travels had equipped them in a way no classroom could. Conversation with them was scintillating and the eligible bachelors (and their parents) found it challenging to match their confidence. Charming looks cushioned with mind and money power made them eminently desirable. The sisters became the talk of the town. Their names too were a matter of curiosity. Aarnavi was one who had a heart as large as the ocean and Anvika meant the powerful and strong one.

At a charity lunch organised by a member of the city's crème de la crème, Aarnavi was accosted by a young man. "Hello," he said, "I've been warned about talking to you because you revel in reducing a man to stammering with your arrogance."

She looked him straight in the eye, allowed herself a half smile and said, "Perhaps your friend can help me with what I can do with someone who is forgetting his manners and etiquette in genteel society."

Understandably, the man beat a hasty retreat. A while later came another man, the lamb to the slaughter. "Aarnavi, my name is Dharam. I am fascinated by your charm and wit. I look forward to listening to your riveting travel tales."

"Hello, Dharam," she replied. "You impress me with your confidence of assuming that I have all the time in the world to entertain you. My calendar is quite full with talk shows that I have been invited to do. Perhaps a travel agent will be able to fulfil your needs."

Joline, aware that her daughters were creating a social stir with their scathing remarks, worriedly told them, "You could be a little kinder to the young men. They are only trying to make conversation. If you don't allow any progress how will you find a life partner? They will be terrified of trying again."

"Don't worry so much, Mamma. There must be at least a couple of stars on the bachelor sky whose shining glory will be irresistible," assured Anvika.

Not entirely convinced, Joline was conscious that her daughters also needed to be equipped with domestic skills and so enrolled them in classes to learn the secret of creating culinary delights. She also introduced them to the delicate world of making fine laces and embroidery. The language and appreciation of Indian classical music was not ignored either. What she had not bargained for was their activist zeal that had been triggered along the way.

Aarnavi and Anvika did not believe in living life on the flyover. They wanted the complete ground level experience. Unknown to their parents, the music teacher, Srimal, masked for the world as the eccentric 'lost in ragas' individual, was in actuality a hard core activist who was a member of a liberation group. He was a crack shot, on the lookout for intelligent recruits who would be dedicated to the movement. In between the *'sthayi'* and *'antara'* of the songs, while explaining the difference, he would deftly include a little anecdote relating to the movement. This would pique the curiosity of his students who would wait after class to listen to some more details.

"Last night we had a very close shave with the police. Somehow they got wind of our activities. We were making hand bombs in an abandoned hut and they surrounded the place. Our friend who was keeping watch sensed that something was amiss and warned us in time. We managed to escape under cover of darkness by swimming across the river. We still don't know who tipped off the police. Trust and secrecy are essential for us along with complete commitment to the liberation movement. Your assistance would be of tremendous help to us in passing messages because of who you are. You are seen as those living in the lap of luxury, close to senior government officials and not inclined towards involvement in any anti-government activities."

Gradually, having won over their confidence and instilled in them a desire to contribute to the movement, he taught them the skill of handling guns and even gave them some practical lessons of how to muffle the sound. This was not just exciting but also immensely empowering for the pupils who had only been exposed to the 'good life'. It gave them importance, involvement and a sense of purpose of achieving a precious dream. There was more to life than making captivating conversation, looking bewitching and setting pulses on a trot.

"How do we get across to you if any intelligence comes our way? Nothing can be revealed to our parents but we are eager to help. It is a little disconcerting thinking of ourselves as spies so I would like to refer to us as intelligencers," said Aarnavi with a mischievous smile but with complete earnestness.

"We have our ways and you will learn soon enough. We need your trust and commitment. There will be visits to libraries where you will place coded messages in specific books, meetings in places of worship to pass on intelligence and also to trusted vendors in markets. But you must continue with your social life," advised Srimal.

Time slipped by and the sisters grew in age and charm. Having learnt to drive they found the freedom to go places on their own, exhilarating. They started attending secret meetings of the organisation and their own reach in the upper echelons of society gave them access to plans being hatched to curtail the liberation fighters. Their lifestyle and societal position would help in keeping suspicion away from them, and they could pass on messages to protect their friends.

Alongside, they also involved themselves in projects for women's upliftment through education, vocational training and even started a newsletter to build awareness of the plight of women and how they could be assisted.

Anvika, at twenty-two, found her shining star in a professor at a well-known university in America who was visiting Calcutta. He swept her off her head and feet and after a whirlwind romance and a preferred quiet wedding, she was sitting on a flight to New York. Aarnavi felt lonesome by her ownsome for a while, having had her as a companion in her escapades all her life. And now she needed her even more as her cover for her budding romance.

Over the years, Srimal and she had become closer and she found in him the perfect partner. Despite her seemingly flittering lifestyle as seen by society, there was in her a hunger for doing something meaningful and with Srimal that was possible—intellectually, emotionally, even spiritually.

They would meet in secret and make music in more ways than one. Willing to be vulnerable and unguarded with each other, the two spirited individuals would be lost in each other's bodies and souls. He was fluid and gentle in his lovemaking and she surrendered to his moves and explorations. She would surprise him with her ability to arouse him in the most imaginative ways and he enjoyed every bit of it. Unfamiliar sensations surged through her and she craved for more.

"I believe I have known you across lifetimes. I love every bit of who you are, even your temper and your moods. Blindfolded I can find the little mole on your thigh and the mark under your breast. You are mine as I am yours. In you I find the strength to continue doing the work I believe in. I would desire nothing more than have you by my side as my wife all the time but my path is ridden with risks and uncertainty. If our movement is successful and we achieve our goal and I can give you more stability and safety, I promise we will get married that day. But whatever the future may hold, know that we will find each other again in lives to come," said Srimal as he held her close, kissing her deeply.

Aarnavi, too overwhelmed with choked emotion, simply clung to him. It was with great reluctance that the couple let go of each other, knowing that they had separate homes to go to. As she drove back home, in a meditative mood, she wondered if she should let her parents know. "Wait for a little more time before talking to them," she told herself, allowing herself a little more breathing time. She knew it would be a difficult conversation and needed to prepare herself.

She went to bed that night lost in the comfort of the thought of being in Srimal's arms. Next morning dawned bright and clear. Winter was on its way out but the morning had a nip in the air. She took a light cover and making herself comfortable with a cup of tea, sat in the verandah to read the newspaper. The breeze froze around her and she could not breathe. The headlines screamed that a few suspected liberationists had been killed in an encounter the previous night. Srimal was one of them.

It was a wooden Aarnavi who went around living her life after that. Her life force had been snuffed out and she merely existed. After a month she also discovered that she was with child. Every fibre in her being was bursting with life and joy. Her Srimal lived in her. Yet, he was gone, her parents did not know and society was unforgiving and cruel to a bastard child. She did the only thing that she could do—sat her parents down and told them, also making it abundantly clear that she was not going to abort the child.

It was a startlingly mature and understanding set of individuals she discovered that day in her parents. "Give us some time to think over the matter. As you can understand it is a shock for us. We live in a society and there are some norms. But we can also see your strong feelings," said her father. Her mother held her close and cried softly, but did not admonish her. She knew her child.

After weighing the options it was decided that closer to the time Aarnavi would shift to the family country house and have her baby there, away from the prying eyes and tongues of Calcutta. "We will need to give the baby to a good orphanage and you must not meet the child after that. The babies from this orphanage are adopted into good loving homes. You will know that Srimal's child is being looked after," suggested her father.

And that is what happened. A baby girl was born and sent to the orphanage and Aarnavi came back to the city. She realised that this was the best option available and was happy she had not lost Srimal altogether, knowing that somewhere his child was growing up. Even Anvika was not privy to these developments.

A few years later Aarnavi met Shekhawat, a businessman, some years her senior, "I am a great admirer of your keen business acumen and would be honoured to start a joint enterprise with you if you accept my proposal." Mellower as a person now, she considered the proposition. Life could get lonely and he seemed a genuine person. "Why not give it a try?" she thought to herself. "We will meet and discuss the details over coffee," she proposed. The business deal did not materialise even after numerous lunches and dinners.

"I don't want to lose you from my life. Please allow me to make another proposal. Will you marry me?" asked Shekhawat, clutching her hand. Her love Srimal, lived strongly in her heart and her daughter was always in her thoughts but she had kept the word she had given her father. She knew that this marriage was one of convenience for her. He seemed nice enough and respected her wish to maintain her maiden name. The businesswoman in her crept into all spheres of her life. Her personal details remained safely locked in her body vault.

Anvika visited Calcutta annually but had relinquished all her rights to the family assets. "I am happy to visit home and get thoroughly spoilt. Don't need the headache of managing property and money matters. I have enough of that in the States. My retirement home for seniors keeps me on my toes." Medical issues had prompted her to adopt a child with assistance from her parents. She named her daughter Shephali and ensured that her Indian roots were well nurtured.

Even if Anvika could not travel to India more than once a year, Shephali would spend her summer vacations with her grandparents and her aunt, visiting the factories and trying to understand how it all worked. "Dadu, tell me how you began it all. I want to study engineering and work here." She was equally curious about how her grandparents met and who proposed first. Dadu and Didima would happily regale her with all the details.

Sikander and Joline had aged considerably and were not in good health. It was Aarnavi who was now managing the business. 'Head and Heart—A Woman of Substance' was the cover story on Aarnavi, in the premier business magazine, *Wheels of Fortune*. "A visionary, Basu is known for her bold decisions. With an appetite for taking calculated risks, she has expanded the family business into futuristic planes. Eco-friendly green vehicles, ranging from battery run, plug-in hybrid electric vehicles, hydrogen and fuel-cell cars to those powered by solar energy, have put her company and India on the world map. Not limiting herself to merely adding to her company earnings, she is also the heart and brain behind specialised charitable hospitals for geriatric and paediatric health care for those living on the fringes of society," read the article.

The work pressure was mounting and she needed someone she could trust and who shared her ideals. Shephali had done her Masters in Business Administration and displayed a happy combination of sharp business acumen and a gentle heart. "Ask Shephali to join you.

She is simply waiting for you to say the word," suggested her father.

"I don't want to limit her in any way. She is young and the world is her oyster, Baba," responded Aarnavi.

"At least you can make a suggestion. Then leave it to her. I believe in the power of genes. Hers have manifested themselves strongly." He replied enigmatically with a smile lurking at the corner of his lips.

Aarnavi longed to believe what her heart seemed to say and desire but she was too afraid to ask—for fear of disappointment or perhaps because she was unsure whether her heart would explode if it were true. She merely followed her father's advice and Shephali was only too happy to shift base to India.

"Mashi[2], I was thinking of ways by which we could expand the business. The movement against plastic and the increase in demand for bio-degradable material is a boon for our jute mills. We need to look into other natural fibres. Bamboo, banana and pineapple are good options. We could employ experts.

The luxury automobile business is doing well and caters to a niche market which is growing. Our production capacity is limited. To meet future demands and stay competitive we need to upgrade our infrastructure now. If you agree I could set up meetings with consultants who deal with this."

Aarnavi saw her genuine interest, involvement and willingness to work. She had also noticed that the policy

---

[2] Maternal aunt.

of setting aside a chunk of the profits for her NGO that worked for marginalised women, resonated with Shephali. At least in this sphere of her life she could be at peace.

Shekhawat and Aarnavi had twins, Saika and Aarav. Finance was never a problem and that in some ways became the biggest challenge. Aarnavi's children, much like herself and her sister, grew up in the lap of luxury but with a difference. Her parents had struggled to achieve what they did and never forgot their beginning. "You are the children of rich parents. For us as children luxury meant two new dresses for a big festival. Life can turn a full circle very quickly. There is never any compromise to hard work," she remembered her parents say. The sisters with all their superficial glitter had hearts that beat with the earth.

The parents of the twins differed widely in their views on the upbringing of the children. Shekhawat succumbed to every wish of theirs, however extravagant and unreasonable. "Don't be so tight fisted and demanding. They will need to work all their lives. If they wish to go to London for the rock concert, let them. They are young, we have the money, where is the problem?" were his views. He himself had a weakness for gambling, as his wife soon discovered, and squandered money. It was a blessing that Aarnavi was solely in charge of her business and her finances were her own.

Her parents had passed on and she had no one to share her concerns with.

When the children were older she had tried to give them some responsibilities in her business but quickly realised that their treatment of the employees was creating unrest.

Aarnavi had had several conversations with her husband regarding their children. "I need you to stop spoiling them. I am worried that they will end up with a sense of entitlement and not learn how to work for what they want. I have noticed that they are disrespectful with the employees and alienate them. The other day Saika asked a very senior employee to shut up. They must be checked," she pleaded with her husband.

Each time her concerns were dismissed. "Don't lecture me on how to bring up my children. If I want to spoil them, I will. You are free to do all the disciplining you want. But let me tell you, I will not have you challenging me in front of them. Look where your hard work has got you. You don't even know how to enjoy yourself and you waste your money on the scavengers. When I married you I thought we would have a fun-filled life of high living where we would be the envied power couple in society throwing champagne fountain parties, spending the summer in London and living a life of grandeur. In reality, ours is an existence of the plebeian and your attitude and lifestyle are so stodgy and ordinary. I don't want *my* children to end up with a life like that."

The children picked up his message quickly enough. It suited them.

Aarnavi's heart sobbed quietly. She had met challenges, faced them bravely and dealt with them the best she could. These were her children and she could see that as people she had not been able to raise them the way she would have liked. The cross currents in her home were too strong for her to swim against. She had tried talking to the twins, taken them to places where they could see for themselves the lives people led, shown them how they could combine a life of comfort with being compassionate. Like vanishing ink it left a momentary mark and then it was gone. They were flying in a stratospheric bubble with no worries regarding their future.

"Don't be such a wet blanket, Mom. We know Dad and you are loaded, your business is doing well. Why are you trying to deny us our pleasures and making us feel guilty? After all, life is meant to be enjoyed. It is our luck that we were born into wealth. When the time comes we will get into the act," Aarav tried convincing her. The mother in her, the tigress with her cubs, as her father had explained, was desperate to believe them so she could be convinced that they would be saved from the downfall of their own making but her keen intelligence said otherwise.

She would have to quickly think of other ways to protect her parents' legacy and also save her twins. Her heart-health was fragile. The doctor had warned her. The strong intuitions she had been experiencing regarding Shephali required immediate investigative action. Sikander and Joline Basu's 'scintillating' daughter was alive and kicking once again, with a focused purpose. She also knew her parents well as they did her. She now understood their plan. The tigress was at work. The sand in the hourglass of her lifetime was slipping fast.

The family assembled for the reading of the will in the living room. The dark brown leather sofas and the polished intricately carved Burma teak and mahogany tables, chairs, corner stands, sideboards and display cabinets gleamed in the diffused light from the Belgian chandeliers. Paintings by Raja Ravi Verma in rich textures and hues added to the dialogue in the room. The furniture, art and tapestry shared a chemistry that miniaturised the humans sitting on the edges of chairs, waiting for the verdict.

The lawyer took out the registered will from the sealed envelope and paused for a second before proceeding. The short break was pregnant with suspense. "I Aarnavi Basu leave my house, its movable assets, my businesses to my daughter Shephali. The certified document to prove the matching of our DNA is attached. My jewellery will be divided equally between Saika and Aarav. Apna Bhavishya (Our Future), the NGO, has been established as a trust. Saika and Aarav will be given a monthly salary for their contribution to the running of the organisation. The details are clarified in the trust deed. Instructions have been given to the lawyer to pay for the higher professional education of Saika and Aarav with the belief that once qualified they will be in a position to build their own future. The property of my husband Shekhawat Sinha is his to give as he may desire. Shephali has no right on that." Other than this there were details of the money left for the trusted and loyal house help.

Silence blared through the room. The tension of the nerves snapped audibly. "What absolute nonsense is this? She must have lost her mind," yelled Aarav. Saika was stunned into muteness. Only her eyes turned towards Shephali and screamed hate. The will had been written and signed by Aarnavi in her complete senses. Shekhawat's allegations of a 'stodgy and ordinary' life led by his wife mocked him. Her absent presence loomed large. Even in death she had curated the script. Old habits die hard.

13
Ancestors

"Stop treating your ancestral jewellery like FMCG[1] products! I cannot understand what it is with you youngsters these days. Use and throw. Your mantra for everything in life—your heart, your relationships, the furniture, your job, your home—the animate and inanimate—all fall in the same category. This fear of missing out on life syndrome is driving you to becoming a nervous wreck. Sometimes I feel your generation in your social strata have undergone mass hypnosis or mass programming. The only consistent features in your life over the past eight years, of your creation, have been your phone number and your email address. And, of course, how can I forget all your plastic face masks, your social media accounts."

"Calm down, calm down, Thamma[2]. *You* have been there. The stable wicket in my twenty-six years. I haven't exchanged you for anyone else, right?" Ruhi tried jovial reasoning with her seventy-five-year-old grandmother. Her 'go to' person for everything from nursing a broken heart to a quick herbal fix for a sore throat. Ruhi's parents were divorced and she had been brought up by her grandmother. Thamma was not amused with the response.

---

1 Fast moving consumer goods.

2 Paternal grandmother.

"That is kind of you but no one else will ever agree to take on my role even if you bribed them. Who wants to invite stolen sleep, your heart maintenance every time you toss someone or get tossed, giving you assurance about finding your feet each time you quit a job...the list is endless. And now you want to exchange all the fabulous ancestral jewellery for some machine-made labels which you hope will buy you a place in your FMCG social circle—there today, gone tomorrow."

"So, what do you want me to do? Become a laughing stock amongst my friends wearing dinosaur age stuff? They wear these stylish, state-of-the-art statement pieces even for the weddings and I stick out like a misshapen thumb. Come on, Thamma, have a heart," I argued petulantly.

"Call it misshapen or think of yourself as different. How about *you* setting the trend instead of following the herd. Besides, remember when you wear an heirloom you are carrying your ancestors with you, the touch of their skin, the aroma of their feelings and their blessings. How much history, how many stories are associated with each one of them. We all come in so many colours. That is what makes us interesting. You will be surprised. You resemble your great-grandmother. She was known as a trend setter in her time."

She had heard stories about her great-grandmother's unusual beauty and independent views in matters ranging from politics, social prejudices to gender equality. Thamma had been given a lot more freedom than her peers and she had chosen her career and husband, which was unusual in her social circle. Ruhi recalled a chat with her regarding her great-grandmother, Raina.

"Tell me about your mother. You say I am stubborn like her. I know she captured many hearts with her charm and looks."

"She lost her husband when she was in her fifties and had several men becoming her suitors even then. I remember feeling envious sometimes," Thamma had confessed.

"So, you were competing with your mother," Ruhi teased her. "But did she respond to any of them? What had the relationship been like between your parents?"

Thamma gave the question some thought before answering. "Looking back, I can say that they had a respectful relationship. My mother was a dutiful wife and my father took care of her."

"Thamma, you don't have to be so careful with your answers with me. She was such a beauty. It wouldn't be a sin if she enjoyed being the queen bee. Were they very much in love? Was he worried about all the attention she was getting? He was an important man and they had to socialise a lot. How did he handle her strong views when women were normally not so forthcoming?"

"So many questions! My mother gave him no cause to worry. She was least interested in the admiration she received from the men. But she fiercely protected her right to her views and feelings. She was a very private person and loved beautiful jewellery."

Ruhi was sitting quietly, cradling the picture of her precious Thamma, recalling the conversations they had had some years ago. She was now a specialist in jewellery and an author of a book on astonishing 'heirloom' stories associated with particular pieces of ornaments. Putting the picture on her lap, her fingers lovingly curled around an exquisite dream in diamond and rubies. It was a necklace presented to her by Thamma, a few weeks before her eyes closed forever. "This is my favourite and I want you to have it. My mother gave it to me. You will appreciate and value it, I know," she had said.

Ruhi had spent hours playing with it, like a child, thrilled with the sparkle, the clarity of the stones and the impeccable craftsmanship. As her fingers explored the delicate nuances she heard a click.

Startled she looked carefully and discovered that the base of the clasp had opened out and inside was a tiny key, studded with gems. With extreme care and trepidation, Ruhi inspected it. "Such a small wonder. Which lock will you fit into?" Questions summersaulted in her head. Unable to find an answer, she finally went to bed and drifted into a fitful sleep.

Golden fingers of the Sun god drumming on her cheeks woke her up the next morning. Not desirous of leaving the soft warmth of the Rajasthani quilts, she turned the other way. Her sleep laden eyes noticed a sunbeam dancing off the shining brass inlay on the ten-inch square block of wood sitting on the chest of drawers beside the bed. It was as if she was noticing the carving for the very first time though the piece had been lying around for years amongst all the other stuff, mostly belonging to her grandmother.

She reached out and brought it to the bed. Looking very closely she realised that the carvings were in fact in gold, in verse form and in calligraphy. Stunned with this discovery she turned it around and discovered etchings of flowers and leaves in between the lines. And one of the flowers had a small hole in the centre. Unable to temper her thudding heart, she mumbled, "C...could it actually be...?" Leaping out of bed she brought the key to the hole and inserted it...and...it...fitted! Very gently, she turned it and the block of wood eased open.

Ruhi's breath came in fits and starts. Her normally strong fingers turned to jelly as she tried to gather the contents of the box. With determined effort she took out a sheaf of old papers. They were in surprisingly good condition and the handwriting was clear and legible. The top sheet had 'Raina' written on it. And there was something else.

Ruhi felt her pulse quicken. Sitting on a velvet cushion in the box, along with the papers, was a startlingly beautiful stone framed in burnished gold filigree. "You carry your ancestors with you," Thamma had said regarding ancestral jewellery. "And their karma that is absorbed by it."

Ruhi was now completely awake. Mind, body, spirit, and heart.

Unknown to Ruhi, Raina had been an expert jewellery designer. Thamma had never spoken about this skill. Perhaps it was not meant to be discussed.

She held the papers with utmost care and started reading. "I was not simply a designer. That was my public image, the benign bored housewife who dabbled in some handicraft in her abundant free time.

I was, in truth, the invisible leader of a small gang of jewel thieves. I created new designs for the jewels from the ornaments they stole so that they could be resold with impunity."

"What? Really?" Ruhi's eyes opened wide and her hands trembled with this discovery. "I am the great-granddaughter of a jewel thief! What impeccable lineage!"

Had Thamma known this about her mother, she wondered. "We come in so many colours. That is what makes us interesting." Her words came back.

Ruhi continued reading. "This is the most magnificent ornament that I have had the privilege of designing. I simply could not let go of it. The stone is a study in perfection. Created in the womb of the earth with utmost care. But in its purity, I see the blurred reflection of my life. I have marred its beauty. And I cannot live with this burden.

I am writing this as a confession. Ever since I was a child, I had a knack for designing, be it clothes, decorating a room or making trinkets with beads. As I grew older this became a serious hobby and I would get the family jeweller to make small pieces of jewellery for me. Soon it took on a larger dimension and he would get me beautiful stones which I would use in my designs.

I realised later that these were all stolen items but the money and power made me avaricious. I could not be bothered that I was in effect becoming a party to stealing gems. I was hungry for power having been scared of the power exerted over me at home. This was like my secret identity and I loved it. My family looked at it as a simple pastime to keep myself occupied.

I had my cover even after marriage of being the ideal daughter-in-law, conscientious wife and responsible mother. I could always say, if charged, I had no idea or interest about where the gems were sourced from. I was the designista.

But for the first time I felt the energy in this stone. I could sense its vibration as I held it and a shock wave went through me. I cannot lie to myself. I felt guilty about what I was doing. We all know about the mystic power of stones. And this one spoke to me...

I could hear its voice inside as it urged me to step back and take a hard look at myself. What do you feel you need to do now? I knew that it was time to stop."

Thamma's words came back to Ruhi. She asked herself, "Do we really carry the karma of the ancestors absorbed by the ancestral jewellery...so what do I do with this now?"

14

Mrs. Sharma

Mrs. Sharma eyed the sparkling rocks matching all the Cs of clarity, colour, carat and cut, with a hungry longing. The caviar, champagne extravaganza, the night before, at Mrs. Poddar's penthouse, had robbed her of sleep. The discreetly lit greens of the rooftop, fantasies in chiffon and crepe, and the heady aroma of spicy masculine perfumes, laced with the intoxicating womanly ones, had made her giddy with envy. Every female figure had exposed portions of the torso glittering in a hundred hues.

She recalled Mrs. Poddar's hurtful comment, "Oh, Mrs. Sharma. So refreshing to see someone who makes a statement with her simplicity. I wish I had your guts, coming to the party of the season wearing just a simple *mangalsutra*[1]!" All along she flashed the setting of solitaires on her bangle as she gestured.

The words sawed through her troubled heart and teased the green in her bile.

Unlettered in the fluency of the English language, she did not have the confidence to give an appropriate and stubbing response. "I can do without your approval, thank you," were words that stayed choked inside her.

---

[1] A string of gold and black beads worn by a Hindu married woman.

Mr. Sharma turned a blind eye to his wife's discomfiture. He had other avenues where he spent his money, and his wife did not feature on his list of priorities. As the marketing director of a multi-national company, he projected himself as the suave, polished, corporate honcho. Persistent and consistent effort helped him reach his designation, but along the way, success had played psychedelic games with his mind. There were too many temptations, flashing and beckoning. And too little time to savour them. He travelled the globe, lived in fancy resorts, entertaining himself and prospective clients. Home and wife, were the dormant fireplace, eager to light up at his call.

Shanti had picked up the courage one evening to speak to her husband. "I need some money. At these parties I feel I am not appropriately dressed. I want to do justice to your social status."

Mr. Sharma was fuelled with the fire of excessive liquor. "Just expensive clothes and designer jewellery will not camouflage your inadequacies to match up to me or my circle. Every single item in this house I have bought with my money and each has an innate class to it. Unfortunately, you are the only *thing* here that does not match up. I don't want to waste my money."

It was one of the darkest nights in Shanti's life. She had no parents to go back to, and no money of her own. But even in the unforgiving pit of the well, she held her head above water and breathed. Sitting next to the window, she stared into blackness, squinting for a dot of light, till dawn broke.

"Shanti, why don't you visit a counsellor? You don't look well, and I'm sure you'll feel lighter if you discuss your problems," advised her sister, a practical college teacher, teaching nutrition, far removed from the fancy party lifestyle.

The idea triggered a ray of hope. "Yes, I need help, someone who can show me a path, out of this misery."

Shanti found a therapist and poured out her woes.

Her journey was to be a lonely one, a battle she had to wage on her own. She was done being ridiculed and insulted. She was going to be someone. But *how*?

"From what I can understand," reflected the therapist, "you feel a sense of rejection from your husband and the social circle he moves in. Do you have friends you feel comfortable with?"

"Yes, I do. Just a few, and we spend happy times together. But I feel angry with the way these women in high circles behave with me, and the way my husband disrespects me. I need to do something about it. I just don't know what." The emotions spewed out.

"I can understand you are looking for recognition and respect. That will help you build your self-esteem. You mentioned that you spend some happy times with friends. What do you all do?"

Shanti was quiet for a few moments, then replied, "It doesn't sound exciting, and it isn't anything to really talk about, but we all enjoy cooking. They love my culinary experiments, and those are the only fun moments I have. My husband passes caustic comments about my lack of talent in any worthwhile field. I am not a fashion designer, nor a newspaper figure, and don't do high profile charity work. Cooking makes me feel worthwhile. So I cook at my friend's house."

The counsellor listened intently and observed the spark of pride on Shanti's face as she spoke about her culinary skills.

"So you feel good trying out new dishes. It excites and interests you, gives you a sense of fulfilment and also gets you praise and acknowledgement from your friends."

"Yes, I do feel good when they appreciate me. Their families also do the same. When their children have friends over, I go and help out. I love the way the children polish off all the food."

"Can we think of your cooking skills as your personal resource that we can work on? That could be the starting point in what you wish to achieve. You cannot be responsible for your husband's views. But you can be responsible for your own happiness and progress. What do you think?"

Shanti had never considered her hobby as a means or a tool to reach the destination she so passionately sought. It had merely been a happy means of escape from the tension, strife and drudgery of her mundane life. "Well, I've never thought of it that way. But now that you mention it, it is something I know I'm good at and feel confident about. But how do I go forward?"

"Now that we have decided on where to begin, I'm sure you'll be able to take the second and third steps. This much I can say. Very few people are fortunate to earn money and fame doing something they love and enjoy."

And so began her voyage.

Something came alive in Mrs. Sharma. Unwilling to ask her husband for any support, she pawned her wedding jewellery for capital. Her sister, who lived by herself, was relieved that Shanti had taken the initiative to start a venture and gave her free access to her kitchen. She named her outfit 'Our Passion Food' and started getting small orders, which soon won rave reviews. Her sister initially got her regular clients amongst her colleagues who were only too happy to get home cooked, tasty food for lunch. The demand, volume and range of items multiplied.

"We cannot limit ourselves to word-of-mouth advertising. I have a friend who can help us with spreading the word on social media. We need to be more aggressive if your dream has to materialise," encouraged her sister. Her assistance proved invaluable. Along with her teaching, she was now an active partner in her sister's enterprise. She dealt with the customers while Shanti preferred remaining in the background. She still had a long way to go. They had employees now who also did the cooking to cope with the demand.

Many items on offer were Shanti's signature products, and she could cater to the palates of all ages. The horizon of her destination did not appear to be just a fantasy anymore. She was getting there!

The magma chamber inside Shanti, that had been silently brewing for so long, was now ready to surface. The break of each morning, brought with it fresh ideas and challenges. Challenges set by her, to raise her own bar. She ploughed back her earning into developing her skills further. There were courses being offered, of specialised world cuisines, and she was an eager and enthusiastic student.

Mr. Sharma had no inkling of her growing strength and popularity. He had noticed that she seemed to be spending more time out of the house but it kindled no curiosity in him. As long as she let him be and took care of the house he could not care less.

Shanti visited her therapist to thank her for helping her untangle her confusion. "You look different and in a happy way," smiled the therapist.

"I certainly feel like a new me," replied Shanti, enthusiastically.

"And what does the new person look like?"

"Like a child who has entered a specialty toy-shop with a blank cheque book, and does not know what to choose!"

"So the older version of you was searching for at least one option when there seemed to be none around. The new you is being inundated with choices."

"I don't want to be just another name on a search engine doing catering. I want a special niche for myself," came Shanti's confident response.

"And what is that?"

"I am attracted to tribal cuisine. They can sometimes create magic with so little, not using any fancy, expensive ingredients. Yet, they are nutritious and tasty."

"So you want to explore the recipes of different tribes. And will that make you happy?"

"That is one part. I have been thinking. Once I am sure I will share it with you."

"You have a plan. I will be waiting to hear from you."

With a fresh spring in her step and a lilt in her heartbeat, Shanti went home. There was work to be done. With the current focus on organic food, Shanti and her sister researched the wholesome millets, seeds, herbs, roots and local plants that went into the recipes.

The sisters travelled to explore different areas, to get a first-hand understanding. Initially they introduced a single dish in the menu that had its origin in the homes of a tribe in an Indian forest. Once it was well accepted they got more adventurous and with time laid out entire tables with food from remote tribes. Shanti experimented with drinks with a difference, made from millets, varieties of unpolished rice and natural sweeteners and spiced them with herbs. There was no stopping her.

Her husband was travelling three weeks a month on work and was relieved that Shanti had a travelling partner in her sister. He did not feel in any way obliged to take her on a holiday. Yet, there was a growing curiosity in him about what seemed to be keeping her busy and yes—happy.

And there was more. The intoxicating glamour that had been one of the perks of his job, no longer attracted him. He looked forward to going back to the stability and comfort of his home. Strangely enough, there were days when he got back early from work expecting Shanti to be around and not finding her there got him irritated.

"Am I getting old? What is happening to me? Why should I care if she is out? Could it be...could it really be that I am missing her? Her quiet calm presence has got under my skin. Unconsciously I have become dependent on her while she needs me less and less..." Mr. Sharma was confused.

The sisters got busier with each passing day. Shanti informed her therapist about having inherited a legacy they wished to continue. Their grandfather had set up trusts to sponsor deserving students from economically challenged families. The sisters put aside money for healthcare and education amongst tribals and set up a separate kitchen to provide hot meals to the homeless in four shelters in the city.

Six years had gone by. The party season was on in full swing. Mr. and Mrs. Poddar were the hosts once again. Only this time it was their wedding anniversary, and Mr. Poddar had made all the arrangements. He wanted to give his wife a rest from all these duties and enjoy a special treat. Silks, crepes, *tussars*[2], top-of-the-line perfumes, exquisitely cut gems and jewellery, ensnared the eyes and nostrils once again.

Finally, it was dinner-time and the spread on the table was to die for. The guests went back for two or more helpings, flinging aside all considerations of calories and 'food pecking etiquette'. There was a buzz about the unusual menu and the quality of the food items.

Mr. Poddar made his announcement. "Ladies and gentlemen, I can see that you are all relishing the food. Let me introduce to you the creator of this buzz. You all know Mrs. Shanti Sharma, but did you know her secret identity—as the lady behind 'Our Passion Food'? I had experienced her cooking skills at a friend's and had

---

[2] A variety of silk.

decided immediately to ask her to help me out when the occasion arose. Little did I know that it was our own Shanti. It was by sheer chance that I met her personally when I visited her kitchen to do a tasting before choosing the menu.

The secret to anyone's heart is through the stomach, as the saying goes, and perhaps Mr. Sharma knows it best, though he humbly keeps quiet about his wife's fine skills. Let's all give her a big hand, and I want to personally thank her from my wife and me for giving us such a memorable feast.

There is one more announcement. She is not only an excellent and innovative chef, but also a great entrepreneur who has gone beyond the lure of amassing wealth to spreading it for the benefit of society. The details of her work will be revealed later at a function where our company has decided to award her and support her cause. And the icing on the cake is that our marketing director Mr. Sharma will present her with the award!"

Mrs. Poddar looked distinctly uncomfortable. Mrs. Sharma, once again wearing a simple *mangalsutra* and a sari, hand-woven by a tribal weaver, knew that no diamonds could win her this sense of achievement or respect. And Mr. Sharma? His visage was a sight to behold!

There was pin-drop silence in the car till they reached home.

And then came some quiet words from Mr. Sharma. A grudging acceptance of his inability to understand, appreciate and value her qualities. "Shanti, you never told me about all this. I could not imagine your cooking would make you so famous. And you have done so much more with it."

Shanti wanted to lash out. "You were so right, though in a reverse way. I don't need expensive clothes and designer jewellery to do justice to me. Actually they hamper my style because they make me feel ordinary and flippant. And yes, I am the only *thing* in *your* house that does not fit in."

But she would not be the kind of feminist who killed the femininity in her. She had her own grace and style. Shanti looked at her husband and answered, "Actually, I have you to thank for helping me find myself. You were disappointed in my ordinariness and expressed it. It hurt me and also made me determined to make a life of my own. I have bought my own place and will be moving out. If you wish you are most welcome to come and join me there."

15
The Confetti

Zaira stood at the corner, utterly distraught. The evening traffic swirled around her, drawing crazy patterns on the pitch black tar as the coloured neon lights bounced off the speeding tires. That evening, Zaira embodied the madness that surrounded her, the impossible pressure to perform, the fearsome burden of success and the dreadful fear of losing the touch. "I have lost my flair for fashion," she moaned as sheer agony wrenched her entrails.

In front of her gleamed the revolving glass prism of the nirvana of haute couture where the chosen few had attained enlightenment. They had created and caused sensations that had walked and talked the epitome of fashion. And Zaira was one of those select few.

But, she had suddenly drawn a complete blank. No ideas, absolutely none, no visions had flickered across her 'inner eye'. She felt dry to the bones. The harder she tried, the more wretched she felt, leading her to dwell in an abyss of nothingness.

Hair dishevelled, and cheeks smudged, with the dripping mascara and kohl, the pitiful figure slowly trudged home as the evening frenzy ebbed into the mysteries of the dark shadows.

"So what are all these theatrics about?" queried Leone, Zaira's live-in boyfriend of two years. "Just quit all this wailing and explain what the problem is. Only then can we find some light," he said in his typical head-over-heart manner. He had no time for what he called Zaira's "eyelash-stretched-to-evening-gown attitude".

Zaira sobered up a wee bit and answered, between sniffles, "I just wish you had a little more heart," and was met with a metallic stare. Unfazed, she continued, "I have lost my wand, my magic wand—the one that simply and effortlessly sprung out of my fingers every time I touched a piece of fabric. Cuts and tucks, slits and slats, ribs and hems, necklines and waistlines all happened so spontaneously—as if the material were conversing with me, whispering its flowing dreams that I was there to actualise. This afternoon, I was handed a gorgeous ream of shaded silk in hues to die for and as I shut my eyes and placed my fingers on it, nothing happened! My mind was a block of hard stone, unmoved and untouched. I became frigid." Saying this she wept a puddle.

"Oh, just shut up, will you?" was Leone's curt response as he handed her a bunch of tissues. "Perhaps you are tired and have overworked your creativity. It is a sign of protest. That to me seems the most reasonable and likely cause."

Zaira was far from being comforted. "How can you be so insensitive? Don't you understand? I've lost *me*—how I define myself—my identity as an artiste—my confidence as a visualiser—the one who can turn the ugliest duckling into a star with a snip and a snap," whined Zaira.

And so the argument continued until both collapsed into sleep. A disturbed night broke into a disturbed dawn, with neither having forgiven the other for the caustic outbursts. Both jumped out of two opposite sides of the bed, and neither uttered any greeting. For Zaira, the problem loomed large and ominous. What was she to do?

Flamboyant yet chic, weird yet elegant, sometimes outrageous yet harmonious—all apparently dichotomous—these were the signature traits of Zaira's concoctions. As she dressed herself that morning, after her typical breakfast of coffee, croissant, and one fruit, she could not put herself into anything stunning. "Liquid in flow yet solid in appeal," the latest review of her works had said. It replayed in her mind as she struggled to put together a head-turner. Finally, slipping into a simple tee and jeans, with large sunglasses to hide her puffy eyes, she stepped out. The cold air stung her cheeks as she walked aimlessly for a while finally heading to the solace of a chapel to sort her confused head.

The flickering embers of the candles cast shadows on the walls of the chapel. Putting her sunshades in her bag, Zaira knelt on the stand and looked at the altar for direction. A storm raged in her mind. Had she been bewitched? Was she a victim of some evil eye, jealous of her success? Had a divine gift been retracted, for some action of hers? Was she being punished for something like her arrogance of belonging to that exclusive club? She waged an internal war, with defendant and prosecutor fighting it out bitterly.

As silent sobbing wracked her, she felt a cool, gentle touch. Startled, she looked up into the kind eyes of a silver-maned lady. "Don't worry, child. Whatever is troubling you cannot be bigger than your existence. Go home, rest, have a nice hot drink and the answers will come. Your struggling now is getting you nowhere." The unexpected warmth comforted Zaira's troubled mind and lit a lamp of hope.

"I am struggling, but I don't know with what. Yes, I have run out of ideas for designing new outfits, but having sat here in silence for a while, I think there is something else that is the real problem."

"So you have already made some progress, my child. Let's take it from there."

"Could we please talk for some time? I don't want to intrude on your time."

"I am here with you to talk if you wish to. Don't worry. You are not intruding."

"For a while I have not been able to sleep properly. I wake up frightened, from my dream, as if something integral to me is being snatched away. I have no power to fight and am helpless."

"How old are you when this is happening in your dream?"

"Around seven or eight years old. I am not entirely sure but I have a very severe looking person around me. She disapproves of a lot of things I do. She does not let me play outside, in case my clothes get muddy. I love getting wet in the rain and splashing in the puddles but she drags me inside and is unkind and says horrible things. I love hugging my dog but she says they carry bugs and so I should not go very close to him."

"Can you describe this person to me? What else does she do?"

"I lost my mother when I was six. This person is the nanny. Her name is Julia. She was brought in to look after us. Father had to run his business and so was often travelling. My younger brother and I had to call her Miss Julia. She was not so strict with him. 'He is a boy and boys don't need to behave like a lady does. He will grow up to be a man and must be rough and tough.' I was not even allowed to dance at will. It had to be structured like during the dance class or when I was practising. I hated it."

"Yes, I understand. You were feeling very controlled and were not free to do simple things that you enjoyed. You also mentioned something close to you being snatched away. Do you recall what it was?"

Zaira closed her eyes for a few moments and then said, "I think I can. It was a cloth doll presented to me by my mother on my third birthday. Even at that age I loved dressing up my doll. I named her Happy. She had a lovely, cheerful smile and my mother and I spent many wonderful hours together making dresses for her. We looked at magazines and then we would draw the outfit. Sometimes we would think up designs and then make the dress with little scraps of cloth we would get from the tailor."

"Who took it away from you?"

"One afternoon when I got back from school I could not find Happy. I looked everywhere. Later, Julia told me that she had thrown away 'the piece of rag'. I had washed the doll many times, and would play with her every day, so she did look old and a little ragged. But I loved her as she was. Julia had replaced her with a new doll when she understood that I was very sad, but it was never the same. It was as if a part of me had been discarded, rejected and thrown away."

"What did you enjoy doing most with your doll?"

"She was like a little baby for me and I loved dressing her up for all kinds of occasions. It could be a birthday party, or a fancy dress, or when she would go out to play, even a school uniform or if she was going out for a formal function. We had so much fun together imagining situations and I would talk to her and I felt she responded. She was my inspiration to be creative in different ways. Sometimes I was her mother, sometimes her teacher and at other times her friend or even her doctor."

"So, what did you do when you found that Happy had been taken away from you?

"I was sad and angry but there was no way I could get her back. No one understood my unhappiness. Not even my father. I felt that I had failed to protect Happy and keep her safe. But since I was just a child there was no action I could take. I just refused to eat for a day and locked myself in my room but that did not help getting her back. I just gave up designing any outfits after that because my Happy was not with me. I lost the interest and then I think lost the talent too."

"Looking back today, do you believe that it was your fault that she was discarded by an adult who was unkind and insensitive? Were you responsible for Julia's actions?"

"No. How could I even imagine that she would do something so cruel when I was not at home? I loved

Happy and looked after her as well as I could when she was with me."

"When you grew up you continued with your passion for designing clothes and making people look nice and feel happy, wearing an attire perfectly suited for the occasion. You had not lost the talent or the interest. It was your hurt and pain that made you feel that way. So do you think you kept Happy alive in your memory and in your daily life by creating beautiful outfits for your clients and being their mentor?"

"Oh. I never thought of it that way. It was Happy who had inspired me to push myself to experiment with all kinds of designs and it gave me a lot of joy too."

"Yes. So as an adult who were you experimenting with instead of a doll?"

"My clients! They had become my dolls. That is such a unique thought."

"And is there a Miss Julia around to take your adult dolls, your clients away from you? You are an adult too now, and do you believe you are in a position to protect yourself and your clients?"

"Of course, I am. I am fully responsible for my actions now and no one can forcibly take away my client or my inspiration from me."

"So, how does this thought make you feel about your anxiety of having lost your touch and your magic wand? If the wand is inside you, can someone take it away? Also, Happy is inside you. Can anyone take her away? How do you think she will feel if you suddenly stopped designing new clothes for her?"

"She will feel dreadfully bored and upset wearing the same clothes all the time. Happy will also feel hurt if I neglect her. She is used to being stylish and she sets the fashion."

"So Zaira, what do you think you should do, now that you are an adult and not helpless as you were when you were a child? Your path is clear in front of you. Just walk on it as you choose, free and confident of yourself."

"Thank you so much for opening my mind and my inside. I feel so much better and surer of myself. I realise I don't have to be frightened of anything being snatched away from me. Julia does not have any power over me now. I am my own mistress and a designer who I am very proud of."

There was no response to her words. Zaira turned around to look for the kind lady but there was no one in sight. The aisle of the chapel was empty. She could still feel the cool touch of the fingers on her forehead and the gentle questions rang in her ears. Strangely, Zaira did not feel uncomfortable with the experience. It was as if she had been conversing with someone known to her for years. Someone who loved her and whom she loved. Who could it have been?

The answer came to her naturally. Of course, she recognised who it was. It was her long lost companion, Happy, who had come to her rescue, to assure her that she had always been by her side and would continue to be there.

Time ticked slowly that morning for Zaira as she processed what she had just experienced. It was a comforting and reassuring feeling. She put herself together, smiling to herself, and walked out of the sanctity of the stone walls, to join the throbbing multitude. She was at peace with the world and herself. With no desire to go to work or return home immediately, she sat in a sidewalk café with a cappuccino and observed the world around. Not having done this in years, she found herself growing interested in the activities around her.

A middle-aged, whiskered man whose moustaches drank more coffee than he did, an earnest young man feverishly painting a masterpiece on the sidewalk, the young lady playing hard to get as the puppy-eyed boy tried desperately to woo her, a bunch of women tucking into sinful bites and enjoying a joke, the lone ranger smoking a pipe and savouring it in complete bliss with his eyes closed, a group of college kids discussing random topics animatedly, punctuating their talk with high-fives, an elderly couple sitting together contentedly in complete silence, the group of little children melting into fluid easy laughter as they played with a bag of confetti, throwing it up into the air and through crinkled eyes watching the shower of colours descending on them. The infectious simplicity penetrated Zaira's warm-turned-frigid-turned-warm being.

As the confetti twirled around in the soft breeze, dancing waltzes, jives and foxtrots, she felt a tug inside, almost like an unlocking. There was complete abandon in the freedom of the pieces of paper in a multitude of shapes, hues and character. They cared for no rules, diktats or expectations. They were there in an explosion of exuberance and seemed not to take themselves seriously at all. They appeared to be enjoying themselves as much as the unencumbered children, taking life easy and carefree. All seemed right with the world.

Taking in lusty breathfuls and mouthfuls of the aromatic coffee, sweeping away the roadblocks in her mind, she blew warm kisses to the children and with a spring in her step made her way back home, to renew her journey called life.

Leone who was about to go out searching for her, met a chirpy Zaira on the steps. Embracing him she said, "Let's get married! My wedding gown is buzzing around in my head. And would you believe it? I even have your suit and our confetti swimming in front of my 'inner eye'."

Utterly confused but relieved, Leone asked the obvious question, "So what happened?"

"Let's just say I felt like dancing with the confetti!"

16

Angel's Trumpet

It was eventide and the waxing moon cast a silver glow over the semi darkness made deeper by the canopy of the large trees. There was much hullabaloo in the village. Murmurings about Heaven's perfume visiting their land had generated enormous curiosity. The fragrance of the vibrant yellow Angel's Trumpets, flowering for the first time near the mango grove, fringing the forest, had drawn the villagers to it. The intense sweet aroma, carried far by the gentle whisperings of the summer breeze, was heady and they simply stood there, allowing the flowers to play magic with their olfactory senses. Most had their eyes closed in a meditative state, breathing in the experience. Peace prevailed.

Only to be shattered like breaking glass. "Have you lost your mind? You and your stupid ways. And by the way it really hurt, having the mango hurled at me. It is not yet fully ripe and the hard hit just missed my eyes." That was Shimli, flinging her hands and open tresses, pouring out her indignation on Ananto. He stood next to her looking dazed.

Ananto had the reputation that preceded him of a boy always up to pranks. His eyebrows kissed his hairline in an expression of amazement. He then responded angrily, "What on earth are you yelling about? I would rather eat the mango if I found one than waste it by throwing it at you. God knows what you think of yourself, always imagining that people have nothing better to do than be after you. You are no *apsara*[1]."

At another corner of the gathering a similar squabble broke out, with two older men getting into fisticuffs. Each blamed the other for throwing hard mangoes. It took a strong, no-nonsense older woman to separate them and at the same time chide them as one does little children. "You are behaving in an infantile manner, attacking each other. Sort out your problems elsewhere and in a more civilised manner about whether *your* wife is having an affair with *him*. Even those allegations are based only on assumptions and rumours. Also we have enough witnesses here to prove that neither of you broke any mangoes."

The trance of the celestial incense had been broken with these disturbances and the crowd was chattering about the thrower of the missiles. Eyes searched here and there and some scanned the world above. The gathering froze as a tremulous wail escaped the lips of a beholder who had spotted a figure in white on the branches of a large mango tree. It sat still as if listening intently to the commotion.

All interpersonal animosities were quickly set aside and a front united in its fear of an unknown threat, coalesced into a mass of breathless breathing bodies. The scared eyes darted in all directions to see if there was only one or more of this apparition. By now darkness was a charcoal black and the shrouded figure, partially hidden

---

[1] Celestial female beauty.

by the leaves and branches, stood out in its clouded whiteness.

"This is a message to us to set our house in order. Tempting us with this ethereal aroma, we have been brought together to recognise the fissures amongst us and inside us. How quick we are to fight with each other," were the words of wisdom from the self-declared holy man of the village.

"This is the spirit of Naina, sent to punish those who cornered her into taking her own life. Her family was of humble means and her parents could not meet demands placed on them after marriage and we all know what that led to," commented one who had taken a shine on her but never had the courage to tell her his feelings.

"Can't you all see the truth? Ever since the developers have been hovering around the forest and this mango grove, planning on occupying the land, cutting the trees and building a commercial project, there has been an array of inexplicable activity here. Obviously, this is a clear warning to them and us from the spirit of the land," said the young nature activist working in the village.

"I knew this would happen sooner or later. People in this village have been so reluctant to give money for building places of worship. We spend money on the latest gadgets but cannot spare a little for the Supreme Power. This is a reminder for us to not forget our priorities," was the opinion of the local politician.

"I don't agree with any of this. I am sure this is the spirit of Sheroo and his curse will be our ruin. In his last days he needed our support and none of us gave him any—none other than Munna who shared his meagre earnings with him to get him food and medicines. And his faithful dog who never left his side. We were all so preoccupied in our busy lives," concluded the village grocer.

Meanwhile, there was a flurry of activity on the treetop. The white phantom had suddenly become excessively agile and was moving from one branch to the other in what appeared to be a random manner. It seemed to be disturbed. Eight-year-old Mohan, who was keenly following its movements, clapped his hands with delight and enthusiasm. "Dadu," he squealed, calling out to his grandfather, "I know what this is. While you were all talking I was watching it and saw its legs and tail. I think it is a *langur* that has been trying hard to take off the white cloth that it has got entangled in. The poor animal needs our help and has been attempting to get our attention by throwing things at us. That is where the mango came from. I can quickly climb up and see if I can do something to help."

The crowd with its sage and learned members, and their observations, stemming from their own unresolved issues, were struck dumb. It had taken a distraught *langur* and an observant curious child to put them in a pensive mood. Much had been revealed. There was much to think about.

The flowers looked happy in the moonlight as they swayed to the rhythm of the wind.

The next morning, a Sunday, saw the village elders gathered under the pipal tree. Various views were expressed.

"I have been thinking about last evening's incident. So many unspoken issues came up when faced with fear of punishment from a supposed supernatural being. It shows there is guilt hiding in us."

"I agree with you. I could not sleep. Nobody talks about Naina or Sheroo but actually we are all responsible. We did not object in one case though we could see that she was being treated badly and we did not help in the other. I have a daughter and what if she goes through a similar experience and no one is there to protect her?"

"I did not have the courage to speak up last evening. When I was growing up this village felt so much more like a family. Sometimes it was irritating because I did not want so many views but I never felt alone or lonely. I remember falling very sick when I was quite young. My mother had gone to her parents' home because her father was ill. I was looked after by the neighbours. My father could go to work because he knew I was in safe hands. Today, no one wants to take any responsibility other than that of the immediate family. I miss the warmth."

"Punditji actually said something very relevant. It seems this incident happened only to help us realise that things are going wrong somewhere. We need to do something."

"Yes, I agree but what?"

The village headmaster who was sitting quietly, listening to the conversation finally spoke up. "The good thing is we agree about the need to wake up and do something. We cannot do anything about Naina and Sheroo. But we can take steps to not let such things happen in the future with anyone else. It is our land and the young boy talked about the forest and mango grove being under threat. We could start with that...."

A few days later, grandson and Dadu ventured to the mango grove, anticipation skipping along with Mohan, looking forward to enjoying the divine aroma once again. But...the Angel's Trumpets were nowhere to be found. Only a handful of faded flowers lay strewn on the ground. Intrigued, Mohan asked his grandfather, his forehead creased, "Dadu, where could they have gone?"

The silver-haired man patted his grandson's head gently and with a smile and a faraway look replied, "Their job here is done. They have blossomed where they are needed now."

17

Close Encounters

It was 2022, and Meenu Gupta was absorbed in the joyful endeavour of compiling a book of stories from her own life experiences and those around her, for her ten-year-old granddaughter. As she reminisced over a cup of coffee, the memories inundated her eyes. "Did these events actually happen or is my mind playing games with me?" she asked herself. Even her children, the in-between generation, looked quizzical and asked in an incredulous tone, "Ma, are you sure of the facts? You better check with your siblings. It seems like a scene from a fantasy movie." True. Even to her, who had physically lived those moments, it seemed unreal. The world had changed dramatically. The slow and steady pace of the Earth's revolution appeared to have spun tizzily, pulling the far off future into the present and throwing the present and recent past into the archives of ancientdom. The saying, that even the present moment as you breathe it becomes history, struck her hard. Nonetheless, she would do what she needed to. "I need to tell stories, true ones, from the family albums, in the best way that I can—as an ode to my times."

The Gupta family—four children and their parents—loved picnics. Any holiday with clear skies and pleasant weather meant time to get the large cane picnic basket ready. In went the different flavoured sandwiches, munchies, fruits, water, creamy cold coffee in flasks, eco-friendly disposable crockery and of course, a special box of tarts—lemon, walnut and chocolate. Each member had his or her favourite. Another bag had the board games, badminton racquets, shuttlecocks, bats and balls. Permanently lodged in the dicky of the large family car was a garden umbrella, a couple of durries to ensure a comfortable place to sit and some cushions. Seven-year-old Meenu, of slight built, loved her books and she would be prepared with her reading material. Mama Gupta, a writer, would always have some paper and pens in her bag.

After the flurry of getting things organised was over, Papa Gupta would holler in his signature deep timbered, substantial volume voice, "Family ready? Let's roll," and everyone would troop out to the car. It was Mama Gupta's responsibility to do the last minute check to ensure that the door was locked and things were in order. And they were off—endorphins activated.

Mr. Gupta had recently been transferred to Delhi from their hometown Calcutta. It was in the 1960s. One evening, he came home from office and declared, "This time we are going to explore a new spot next to the river bank that has a particularly scenic view. A little away from the city, it has the added attraction of wild peacocks walking around and if we are lucky even get to watch them dance, with the glory of their plumage on display. Some people have also had the privilege of watching nilgais and stray deer grazing on the grassy stretch next to the bank and sharing salad with curious and friendly wild rabbits." The family waited eagerly for the next holiday. It had the promise of being an exciting one. It certainly was and how!

It was October, crisp and cool, early morning and the Guptas were off. After a two-hour-long drive, the family reached their destination and quickly unloaded the goodies and accessories to make themselves at home in the wide open outdoors under the cool embrace of the sprawling banyan tree. The vast blue sky was clothed in wispy white, flowing and floating drapes. Papa Gupta stretched himself on a durrie, head cradled on a soft cushion, breathing in the fresh mossy fragrance and soaking in the feel of infinity as he looked heavenwards. Mama explored around a bit and then joined her husband. The children engaged themselves in a game of badminton and having tired themselves out, settled down to some board games, munching sandwiches, tarts and washing them down with chilled coffee.

"Don't polish off all the chicken sandwiches and leave only the cheese and cucumber for us," warned fourteen-year-old Agneesh as Rakhi, all of twelve, wolfed down her favourite item. "And how about being generous and sparing some lemon tart for me too," appealed ten-year-old Ved, worried at the rate at which the dessert was vanishing. "There is enough and more for each one of you. Just relax everyone," assured Mama, as she shut her eyes in a bid to snatch some beauty sleep. Peace and tranquillity prevailed.

Meenu, the quiet one, lost in her Enid Blyton world and of late the wonderland of Alice, decided to stroll off on her own to inspect the pebbly riverside's unique stones in attractive shapes and colours. It was quite shallow near the bank and the playful gurgle amused her. Multitude of sea shells, collected from the sea shore during their beach visits, dried branches in interesting shapes from the hills, were her treasured belongings. To this she wanted to add the river stones and pebbles, creating her own Nature corner, replete with memories.

Reminisced Meenu, "As the family lazed under the tree, I entertained myself, bending down and picking up polished pebbles in various shades and placing them in my pink frock, the front of which I had folded into a little conical shape. I was engrossed in my activity. Thinking back I can re-live, re-see and re-feel the cool sparkling water lapping gently at my toes as I gingerly stepped a little deeper to stretch and pick up a shining gem. I was thrilled with my collection and wanted to show it off to my family. I stood up and turned to go back when I felt the earth move ever so slightly beneath my feet. Confused, I wondered what was happening when I felt it slide a little more. Looking down carefully, I noticed that I was standing on what appeared to be a... No, it could not be...but it was...a crocodile...with the back half of its body in the sun.

I raised and waved one hand in desperation, trying to get my father's attention, clutching on to my frock with the other. I tried screaming but my voice had shut down. My feet were terrorised lead. I simply could not move. After what seemed an eternity, Dad noticed my peculiar behaviour. He ran towards me asking what the matter was but got no answer. My panic stricken expression fuelled him into breaking the sound barrier. He flew. By now the crocodile was moving faster and I was standing on it, near its tail. Moving like lightning, my father pulled me up and heaved me away towards himself, wrapping his arms around me. The angry crocodile whose sunbathing had been disturbed and who had been denied a good meal, slithered into the water and swam off.

That was the one time I saw my father weeping.

I still have those pebbles, including the shiny one, in my Nature collection, which I will gift to you, my little one, along with this story. If only they could talk."

Certain incidents get etched in one's memory. This particular one had to do with Meenu's grandmother who was living with them for a few years. Meenu was in her early teens and her father was posted in North Bengal. Times were turbulent politically. Under the veneer of normal life there was trouble brewing.

Recalled Meenu, "One evening I went with my father to the grocery shop next to our house and the man behind the counter spoke to my father in hushed tones. 'I have heard snippets of conversation when people visit my shop. A conspiracy is being hatched. High profile families are targets and your family is not safe here. Kidnapping, dacoity and brutal killings are to be expected. It is a well-planned operation and the police may not be able to give you complete protection. I can organise a car to take you away to safety under the cover of night. Discuss this at home and let me know. You have to decide quickly. And remember to trust no one. Stay indoors as much as possible and do not send the children to school for a while. The house help must have no inkling of your plans.'

I remember my father looking very serious and after we came home he took my mother aside and they had a long conversation. Ours was a family known in the area and we had inherited wealth. I understood later that the money was in real estate and gold. My grandmother did not believe in vaults. There were heated arguments with my father trying to convince her to use the facility of the bank locker.

'Modern conveniences are to be used to our advantage and you are only adding to our tension by holding on to this responsibility,' he tried to argue. It fell on deaf ears.

'*Shona*[1], don't get so angry,' she told him. Let an old woman live with her idiosyncrasies. This is how I have seen it being done by my grandparents with whom I grew up. It gives me peace. Life can take unexpected turns. I have lived through strange situations where even your breath turns against you. What if the bank shuts down or we suddenly need access to the things? What if we need to move quickly? I want to have it within reach. When I am not around you can do what you want but for now I have my safe place.'

Her safe place was keeping the precious metal in bolsters, nestled inside the cotton wool!

Matters took a turn for the worse very quickly. Our family had no choice but to escape under the shroud of darkness. True to his word, the well-wisher grocer did his bit and in the dead of night we were bundled into a van with bare necessities like important documents, keys and some clothes.

---

[1] A term of endearment.

AND the Bolsters.

The eighty-five-year-old matriarch looked calm and confident, prepared to face the challenge. The key to our freedom was secure with us.

There had been no opportunity to visit the bank had the gold been kept there. And it was a long time before we could return to our home.

I think the saying 'old is gold' took on a whole new meaning for my father. I remember him putting his arms around his mother, tears moisturising his parched lips, as the car sped away to safety."

Meenu recalled yet another incident that happened soon after she got married. "I was all of eighteen, with minimal exposure to the nuances of human idiosyncrasies, cocooned as I was in the intimate cradle created by my parents and siblings. By now there were five of us brothers and sisters and we were enough and more for each other. We had created our very own planet in the Milky Way galaxy and everything else was considered alien. Our bond was such that we were five bodies and one soul. And it has remained that way. The only change or progression if you would like to call it, is that, over time we have merged our planet with Earth.

My husband was posted in the districts. Our government accommodation was a huge single-storied sprawling house with very high ceilings; the dining room had a spiral wooden staircase from one side going up to a large lobby with a wooden floor; the drive-in to the portico was a good hundred metres; the living quarters for the house help was at another far end and the grounds of the house had innumerable fruit trees, vegetable spots, a large pond and even a paddy patch.

It truly was a world unto itself where time had taken a l…o…n…g siesta. Getting used to having a husband, marriagehood, memsahibhood, running a household was all quite overwhelming.

The house-help who had become a part of the bricks and stones down their years of service, also did not quite know how to relate to me—was I the lady of the house who they needed to take instructions from (considering that they were the ones who were constantly guiding me), the new bride who they felt responsible for, the teenage urban colleen who they had to gradually 'break' into panchayatdom or simply a bewildered, lost young girl who they felt indulgent towards and sometimes even took the latitude to tease and have fun with… Perhaps it was all of these at various points in time. My husband had long hours at work and it was they who became family for me. They and their children. But as with all things this too took time. It was a process and things happened along the way.

One of my first initiation 'ceremonies' was on a morning when I was enjoying a leisurely cup of steaming tea with home-made *nankhatais*[2], by myself, on the long verandah. A couple of parrots and two mynahs were my regular visitors who had adopted me into their fold. They would sit on the table nibbling at the biscuits, informing me, as I interpreted it, about the world events

[2] Shortbread cookies.

as they saw them through their bird's eye view. We were very comfortable with each other and understood each other well.

In this ambling, dawdling, reposeful time capsule, as I savoured a sip of the tea, I glanced at the main gate and my plasma went into frigid mode.

The guard was nowhere in the picture and hurtling down the driveway was a man, wearing only what appeared to be a half lungi, body smeared with mud, eyes bloodshot, face streaked with colour, bare feet, unkempt hair in knots and holding a long iron rod. As his strides vanquished the hundred metres between us, I managed to put down the cup and let out a scream.

The birds, sensing that something was wrong, did not abandon me. Instead, they came closer and two of them sat on my shoulders. It was one of those moments when I felt intensely protected and desperately vulnerable all at once—the play between the mind and the physical body.

'Ramu, *jaldi aao*[3],' I yelled out to the cook, in a quivering voice, mustering up all the strength I could gather. The man was nearly upon us, having reached the portico. Gathering all the courage, dignity and self-respect that I could find access to, I looked at him directly in the eye and spoke sternly, '*Kaun ho? Kya chahiye? Wahin ruko.*[4]' Testing my limits the man gave a smirk and started climbing the steps. I stood up on knobbly knees and was

---

[3] Ramu, come quickly.

[4] Who are you and what do you want? Stay where you are.

preparing to make a dash for the door when I heard muffled laughter.

I could not believe my ears or my eyes. Opening the door were the cook and the bearer and they were both stifling their giggles. How dare they? And then I looked at the stranger and realised that he was standing very demurely and greeting me politely. What was this all about?

Sensing my underlying irritation and my obvious discomfiture and confusion, Ramu hastened to explain things to me. 'Memsahib, don't get angry. We would not allow you to come to any harm. We simply wanted you to experience a tradition in this place of the "*bahrupiya*".'

'I have no idea what you are talking about,' I answered, relieved but still a bit shaken.

'They are just local actors who impersonate people. The fact that you got genuinely frightened means that he played his role well. They create intense drama with their sudden appearances. Often they come dressed like gods or goddesses, policemen, postmen or someone threatening. If they are convincing, people give them *baksheesh*[5]. It means that you are happy with their disguise. This is how they make a living. In olden days, we have been told, if they repeatedly proved that they could fool people with their disguise then sometimes they were even used by kings to go to the enemy camp to try and get secret information.'

This was certainly a learning for me and something I would tell my husband when he got back from office.

---

[5] A small sum of money given as a tip.

For me, in this new phase in my life, each day itself was a '*bahrupiya*', unfolding itself with multiple surprises and teachings."

Meenu continued with her reminiscences. "My life in the district as the wife of an important government official was eventful. As I mentioned earlier, I was naive and untrained in the ways of the world, accepting things at face value. Much like a blank canvas is how I now see my life as it was then, and daily happenings etched a small story that I recall scene by scene, like a graphic novel, vivid and detailed.

After several catastrophic attempts at making '*luchis*[6]' which are supposed to be fluffy, light with a bouncy texture, I decided to stick to making plain steamed rice and even in this mundane venture managed to get the rice grains sticky.

Sheer frustration made me decide to impress my husband by trying my hand at gardening instead, since I knew he loved the fresh vegetables from the kitchen garden and enjoyed the flowers smiling happily in the front lawn. As a child I had been given my own strawberry patch to tend to by my father. I loved putting the baby strawberries on the berets made with straw, placed around the bottom of the plant so that the berries did not touch the ground.

It was June, temperatures were high and we did not have electricity. The high ceilings helped. We were

---

[6] Puffed, deep fried, all-purpose flour bread.

younger, unspoilt by the comforts of life today and possibly global warming had not yet struck hard. Dusk meant that all the hurricane lamps were lit by the house help and each room had one or two, with oil being placed in it to last for a few hours.

My husband was travelling on work and I was to stay by myself for three days. It was a daunting proposition, considering the sprawling house, with the quarters for the house help being at quite a distance.

'Would you like to spend a few days with Mrs. Mitra? She is a senior lady and you seem to get on well with her. Her husband will be travelling too and you two could spend these days together,' my husband suggested out of concern, realising that staying alone might be a challenge for me.

I did not want to appear a weakling and putting up a brave front said, 'Don't worry. I'll be fine. You have many books and I'll use this time to catch up on some reading.'

Of course, I did not feel anything close to being lionhearted but my indomitable ego refused to be compromised. Morning arrived and the official team left for work. I was on my own. There was a thick tome on gardening and I had strategised on covering the first night reading the book. Staying awake helped tackle the night darkness. Eyes open meant empowerment, at least to me.

Supplies had come in from the city of large quantities of dry fruits, nuts and baking paraphernalia. I was going to bake a surprise for my husband to welcome him on his return. There was a book on baking and that was going to take care of the second night along with a romantic novel by Georgette Heyer. I enjoyed her wit and her detailed historical novels.

'Ramu, this evening please make sure that the oil in the hurricane is filled to the maximum so that it lasts the night through. I plan on staying up and reading.'

'Yes of course, Memsahib. I will ensure that you are not left in the dark. Please keep a torch with you just in case you need it.'

I dilly-dallied over dinner, starting late, eating slowly and talking to the staff to try and make the all-by-myself night as short as possible. Eventually they all left, having locked the doors and I made myself comfortable on the bed, armed with a torch, drinking water, the book and the hurricane lamp. It all started well and I was making a sincere effort at understanding gardening skills.

The grandfather clock struck twelve and mentally I counted the number of hours left for the sun to rise and shine on us. My eyes felt heavy but I was determined to stay awake. A drink of water and a few paces around the room ensured that this happened. The trees swaying in the night breeze cast strange shadows inside the room which I refused to 'freak me out' as my granddaughter would say. Things were going smoothly till the lamp started flickering. It was close to 1 am. The table clock told me the time.

The light bobbed up and down as if dancing to some unheard music and my heart jiggled along with it. What if...what if...and whoosh...as if swept away by some gush of wind the light went off. I scrambled for the torch and fumbled to switch it on. The light was feeble and clearly would not see me through the night. It fell in small patches, highlighting parts of objects adding to the eeriness. And then, seemingly set to a timer, peculiar sounds emerged from what appeared to be the dining room. Scratches, pattering, thuds, squeaks—building up to what sounded like a thoroughbred warfare.

I could not distinguish between the thudding of my heartbeat and the other noises—all of which got fused into a cacophony, leaving me gasping for breath. What on earth was going on? Many ghost visitations had been rumoured in these old houses and I had heard some tales of our house too. Whoever, whatever they were—they were in a riotous mood and soon I could hear crashing sounds too. I could not, dared not leave my room which at least till then had been spared of any obvious visitors. Picking up the pillows, I placed them on my ears, much like an ostrich burying its head in the ground, trying to ward off the invaders. The house was under attack and I curled up in bed.

Slowly, very slowly, the deep dark night eased into the pale light of dawn. Exhausted, I somehow dragged myself out of bed and tiptoed to the dining room. It was indeed the remnants of an after-battle ground. The packets of dry fruits and nuts kept on the table had been demolished and were strewn all over the floor and a trail of dry fruits could be seen on the spiral staircase.

What suspiciously looked like wiry tails were hanging from the edge of the stairs. On closer inspection I realised they were indeed the tails of overstuffed field rats that had had a field night and were snoozing after their party. I was unsure of my own emotions at that point in time.

Soon the staff arrived and I immediately quizzed Ramu. 'Why did the lamp go off so soon? I had clearly asked you to put enough oil for it to last the night.' He hung his head in shame. He had obviously not put in enough oil. 'But believe me, Memsahib, I had never even imagined the siege of the field rats. We know rats are very determined and clever and they dig long tunnels under the ground where they store all the food. I am sure that these rodents have an informant that spread the news of the house being easy prey with good food available and they arrived in large numbers using some channel they have secretly dug,' was his response and analysis for whatever it was worth.

The episode was enough to put me off gardening forever even if it meant a lost opportunity of impressing my 'new' husband. Dealing with field rats in the garden was not an activity my heart could handle, having done its thudding vis-a-vis rats for this life and those to come."

There was yet another story from Meenu.

"Despite living in the heartland of rural India or probably because we were living in the districts, where time ticked slowly and interaction with Nature in its myriad faces was a daily occurrence, each dawn brought with it a new curiosity. I remember it was a humid summer evening. Dusk had fallen and since there was no electricity, the kerosene lamps had been lit in the rooms. Unlike an electric bulb which, depending on the wattage, can light up an entire room, corner to corner, a lamp has a rather romantic diffusion of light which gets dim as you move further away from it.

As children, our upbringing had some behavioural norms ingrained in us. Decades later, they are just as alive in my daily routine. As the sun dips westward, I find myself heading cupboard-ward, to take out a fresh set of clothes to welcome the evening. My mother's words ring clearly, 'It is nearly five o'clock. Wash yourself and apply some snow[7] and powder. Change into another dress and go outside to play in the garden. Remember your body is your temple and you must keep it clean and healthy. Otherwise, how do you expect God to feel welcome there? Also, if you are clean and neatly dressed you will feel better and happier.' I have never questioned this logic but it works for me. If I don't freshen up at the end of the day I feel lethargic and dull.

The concept of giving '*shondhe*' was also a regular practice. After getting spruced up, the lady of the house would blow the conch in the puja room or in front of the mantle where the deities were kept, light an incense (*dhoop*) and take it around the house, probably to clear out any negative energy. The aroma of the sandalwood incense burnt in our house is very dear to me and I use it regularly too, inhaling and absorbing my happy childhood everyday. It energises and comforts me. Some households also used '*dhuno*', a plant resin giving off aromatic smoke when it is lit for the worship and in the evenings it is reputed to drive away the mosquitoes.

---

[7] Snow was a type of vanishing cream that was not sticky.

So here I was, in my Raj-era home, each room the size of a three quarter badminton court, changed and getting ready to greet the evening. Getting dressed also meant combing and tying your hair, which was usually long, into a knot at the nape of the neck. Leaving your hair loose and flowing like a cape was not an option. To secure the hair well and tight we used a sturdy black chord to first make a pony tail.

I had misplaced my chord and was searching for it all over the house. The lantern light was lost on the greyish floor. The sky deepened to highlight the lone star and daylight was snuffed out. Near the large door of the drawing room, opening into the long verandah skirting the house, I noticed my chord lying on the floor.

Relieved that my mane would now be neatly fastened, I bent to pick it up and was jolted into stopping by a terrified scream from the back. 'Memsahib, stop! Don't touch it. Step back quickly. It is a snake and an extremely venomous one.'

That was Ramu, ashen faced and totally shaken. His eyes were shining with unshed tears of horror and relief. He rushed to get the potable lamp closer and sure enough, inspection revealed that it was a black krait. 'It has made its way into the house probably looking for some dry comfortable place to relax since there have been a couple of showers. It is usually more active at night,' he explained.

I must confess I had not had such a close encounter with a snake earlier and the near-touching-it experience gave me the cold sweat jitters, leaving little real estate in me to be particularly interested in getting a lesson on krait preferences or psychology. Between Ramu and the other staff members, they managed to remove the reptile and let it loose in its natural habitat but ensured that all the doors and netted windows of the house were bolted and barred.

I will also admit that whatever angst and hurt I might have been harbouring with reference to Ramu for having put me through the ordeal of the *bahrupiya* and field rat episodes, saving me from the deadly krait warmed the cockles of my heart. I was ready to embark on an all new chapter in my relationship with him and the others."

The next story is a page from Ramu's life. He was around fourteen when he had been conferred the title of the school first aid expert, a great honour indeed. He took this role seriously and had been a dedicated student, learning all the skills of first aid, living outdoors with minimum accessories, taking care of those in need, especially the elderly. Along with mastering the art of tying different types of knots, to suit the requirement, he had a team of assistants and they would help the villagers, including nursing them when there was an outbreak of cholera.

His father, a peon, moved with his employer to a small town and the family was in the process of settling in. The house had a large garden serviced by two gardeners and Ramu lived in the outhouse with his family. One evening, while tending to an overgrown bush, one of the gardeners felt a sharp prick on his wrist. With a cry he pulled his hand out and noticed some marks.

Ramu, who was close by, ran to him and on examining the hand immediately got busy arranging to tie a tourniquet. His training warned him that it was the bite of a venomous snake and he told the man, "I am tying this for the time being. My father will be returning soon and will take you to the hospital in the bigger town. Don't open the knot even if you feel uncomfortable."

As they waited for the father to get back, the gardener went to his room and disregarding what he thought were the words of a mere child, opened the tourniquet. He was certain that it was simply the bite of a harmless creature. He was wrong. Soon news arrived from the staff quarters that the man was feeling very unwell and was frothing from the mouth. By then another staff member had arrived and he mentioned an *ojha*[8] who lived about ten miles away. Desperate, Ramu and he got on to their bicycles, that being the only mode of transport immediately available, and went off.

Cycling with every ounce of energy they reached the man and asked for his help. This is what he recounted. "The man was tall and wiry. He had a long beard and was wearing just a *dhoti*[9]. He lived in a one-room hut with a small verandah. We gave him the details and begged him to come back with us. He insisted on doing a little puja before leaving and walked off into his room as we waited in the verandah. Impatience and worry drove me to step into his room after a while.

---

8 Healer.

9 Cloth tied around the waist and reaching the ankle, mostly worn by men in India.

What I saw has been a mystery all my life. I believe in logic and this was quite the contrary. The man was seated on the floor, cross legged, in front of the image of a deity under which was a mirror. The room was bare and stark other than one wooden bench that served as a bed and a small table with nothing underneath either of them. He had his eyes closed and appeared to be in deep concentration.

The room had a light and I saw the reflection of a snake appear on the mirror, hood raised. It was alive and moving but there was no actual snake around. I stood there mesmerised as the man slowly opened his eyes and turned around. He looked at me directly in the eye with a grave expression and said that there was no point in his accompanying us. He had seen the snake that had bitten the man and there was no hope of reviving him. There was a finality in his words and as it turned out he was right. This has been the most bizarre experience in my life that defies all logic yet I saw it with these very eyes."

Things happen. Meenu sat with a faraway look, nursing her third cup of coffee.

18

Gramdida

You could call it an upmarket village, trying hard to gain the status of a small town but not quite there. And in that village, right next to the main road, the only road really since the rest were lanes, was a quaint, one-storied house. It had a terracotta tile roof, attractive exposed-brick-finish walls with large windows and a large verandah with lush green foliage on all sides of mango, jackfruit, coconut, guava, litchi and date palm trees. A haven for birds. And for the children of the village who were occasionally allowed to pluck some ripe fruits.

In it lived a woman, an old woman with sparkling black observant eyes, soft translucent skin, wispy-silver-hair tied into a knot on her neck and a kind smile that penetrated hearts, especially troubled ones. Her ears patiently listened to the happenings in the lives of those passing by and talking to her. Her mind and heart engaged with them with the combined wisdom of lived years and love.

No one knew her exact age. It could have been anywhere between seventy-five to ninety. Not that it bothered anybody, least of all herself.

Most of her waking hours she spent on her recliner in the verandah. Next to her chair was a sturdy table. The top of this was regularly serviced by a young tribal girl,

Chameli, the house help, with tea and biscuits, fruits garnished with rock salt and a dash of lemon, meals and the occasional sweet.

In the season paced life, where the changing moods of the sky, the blushing blooms and fading falls of flowers and leaves, thundering showers and scorching heat, the seeding and harvesting, mellow winter sunbeams and bright summer sunshine made up the calendar of life, it mattered little how many times the earth had circled the sun.

What did matter was whether the seasonal crop had been abundant, medium or poor.

Whether the tiny buzzing tea stall next to the giant pipal tree gave the same quality more milk and less water, boiled tea, with cardamom, ginger and other spices or black tea with pepper, lemon, black salt, sugar being added to individual taste. Morning was the time for *luchi* with a potato gravy and thin *jilipis*[1] and evening was reserved for *shingaras*[2] and onion *pakoras*[3]. This was where the village-aspiring-to-be-town inhabitants met to share their woes and joys and discuss threadbare the world happenings. Timings were clearly demarcated for the morning walkers, mid-morning house-work-completed women's group, stray non-siesta afternoon goers and the evening was a potpourri of all sorts.

---

[1] Jalebis—crispy fried spirals made of rice and gram flour, which are then steeped in sugar syrup.

[2] Samosas—seasoned potato stuffing in a thin flour wrap that is fried.

[3] Onion fritters.

And what mattered was whether the local politician was insecure enough about winning the next election to carry on with his welfare measures like setting up a good healthcare centre, building and maintaining the road and upgrading lanes, ensuring clean drinking water and regular supply of electricity, making sure that the government school functioned and the teachers did their job.

What got curiosities accelerated was, "I have heard that Narayanda has another wife in the city where he goes regularly for his business. They even have a son. He has bought her a fancy house. She is supposed to be quite an eyeful and used to be the companion of the local zamindar. I wonder if Romadi knows. Even if she does, what can she do—poor thing, she has no place to go to and there are the twins to look after. I think her in-laws know because they are unusually nice to her."

And then there were the family secrets. "Don't tell anyone but the Saha family has a curse on them. All the sons have had failed marriages and so there is no grandchild. Someone has done some black magic because of jealousy since they were so prosperous. Have you heard of '*vashi karan*'? It is a kind of spell to control someone or a situation. Believe me, it works."

"How are you so sure? Have you tried it?"

"Of course, I have. Otherwise, how can I be so sure? I got it done on my husband to make sure that he was in my control, did not look at any other woman and was completely dependent on me. I handle all the money in the family. I was scared he would waste it on his brother's family."

The new bride gossip was ever popular. "Maya, who works for the Ghosh household, also works for me. She told me not to tell anyone but I am sharing it only with you. The new bride sleeps till nine o'clock and expects tea to be served to her in bed. Her husband, feel sorry for him, has to bring it to her. And shamelessly she wears her nighty in front of her father-in-law."

"Just the nighty?"

"I asked Maya the same question. Sometimes she wears a housecoat but often just the nighty and you know it can be transparent."

"Can't her husband or mother-in-law say anything?"

"I think they are scared. Her family has high connections and the belief is that they can make trouble. Mr. Ghosh has been given favours for his business by them. That is why he agreed to the marriage even though the bride is so ordinary to look at."

Gramdida[4] of the terracotta tile roof home, as she was affectionately called, had her finger on the pulse of all the gossip and the village shaking events, though she barely stepped out of her home. News reached her through her daily visitors who dropped by for a cup of tea and a chat. She also had access to what could be termed classified information.

It was a regular morning in the village. And Gramdida was following her regular routine. After having completed her morning rituals, she strolled in her garden plucking

---

4 Village grandma.

flowers to offer to her Gods, sprinkled seed for the parrot and mynah families that breakfasted with her and then settled to have tea on the recliner, which had comfortably shaped itself to her dimensions.

The morning had lulled itself to a rhythm when the wrought iron gate was opened with jittery nervous energy by a distraught Romadi. "Dida, I hope you are not expecting anyone. I need to talk to you and it will take some time," she said, walking up the steps of the verandah and pulling a chair for herself.

"You look worried, Roma. We can talk and if someone does come we will continue the conversation later. Not that I am expecting anyone in particular," replied Dida.

Her understanding tone was enough to unlock the floodgates of unshed tears and Romadi buckled up, using her sari to soak the deluge. "I am being punished for my sins and I need to tell someone. It is killing me inside. No one talks about it openly but I know that my husband has a mistress. She also has a son to whom he is going to will all the property. But this is all my fault." And saying this she burst into another weeping episode.

Dida sat quietly, simply holding the space of her grief and anguish and allowed her the luxury to cry unashamedly till she quietened down. She then called out to Chameli to refill the pot of tea and get some biscuits. "I can see that you have not eaten this morning. You will feel better after a cup of hot ginger tea."

"I was desperate to get accepted by my in-laws' family. Even after five years of marriage we did not have a child and they were planning on getting him remarried. Everyone blamed me. I could not go back to my parents' home because they had made it clear that after marriage I had to adjust to my new home and there was no place for me in their house. I did whatever I could to bear a child. I went to a well-known doctor in the city who started treating me but my husband refused to get a check-up.

I also visited a *tantric*[5]. He told me that the only way to appease the Gods was by sacrificing a child. Nothing else would work.

I fell under his spell and even got intimate with him because he said that would complete the process. He gave me the assurance that everything would be fine and I felt accepted.

He did not judge me or tell me that I was suffering for something I had done in my previous life. I sold some jewellery and gave him the money to buy a baby girl whom he sacrificed in a secret ritual. And I am being punished for all these horrible sinful acts of mine. I have two daughters and have lost my husband to the other woman anyway. Believe me, Dida, I have not had a single night's peaceful sleep all these years. I keep thinking about the little girl and don't know what to do."

"We will have to think of something, won't we?" responded Dida, after processing what she had heard. And she had a lot to process as it triggered long buried memories. Very few people (and no one in the village) knew the story of Dida's life. Married at the age of sixteen or so, after completing school, into a well-to-do family, she had lost her husband a year later. She had barely

[5] Shaman/mystic.

met him since he was out at sea working for a shipping company. News reached the family that he had been stricken by an illness of the heart and death was quick. He was in his twenties.

Labelled as a bad omen for the family, Dida lived at the mercy of her in-laws. Other than her long hair being shorn off, she was compelled to wear only white saris and not allowed any non-vegetarian food, not even onion or garlic lest it agitate and activate her hormones. It was a permanent life of mourning (and punishment) for someone whose face she struggled to remember.

Years later, she had spoken out her feelings to a young research student who was chronicling the life of young widows in the earlier days with the understanding of maintaining strict confidentiality regarding names. "I would longingly see my sisters-in-law who were my age, wear bright vibrant colours and when no one was looking I would take a colourful lustrous silk sari and place it against my face and see myself in the mirror. It was one of the few saris that I had hidden, belonging to my trousseau.

All my activities were watched with hawk like eyes, lest I 'indulge' myself in any way. Fond of dancing, my feet would involuntarily tap to the beat of a rhythmic song and would be given long disapproving glares by the elders in the room. I would watch others enjoy fish and mutton, the taste of which I loved. There was a little five-year-old girl, my niece, who noticed what was happening and she would come into my room in the afternoon and give me some chicken, fish or mutton. It is amazing how she could understand my feelings and never told anyone what she was doing. When young men, friends of my younger brother-in-law visited, I wanted to look pretty and talk to them but it was not allowed. My entertainment was going to the puja room and spending time there to cleanse my mind of all evil, sexual thoughts."

Life was a drudgery and Dida kept busy with work around the house for the next five years or so. Reading story books from the house library in the afternoons was her only escape and a powerhouse of inspiration. An intelligent, spirited girl, life situations had robbed her of her agency and she had nearly forgotten her zest for life.

One night, in the slumberland of dreamless sleep, she felt a warm, alcohol ridden breath next to her face. Terrified, she opened her eyes to see her elder brother-in-law forcing himself on her. "W...wh...what are you doing...stop...stop..." She tried to scream and his heavy paw like palms pressed her mouth to stifle her. She did the only thing she could. Mustering up all her strength she bit into his hands. He yelled in pain and that woke up the household who came rushing to her room.

Dida continued with her story to the young researcher, "The scene was self explanatory. My brother-in-law's wife was livid and mortified, all at the same time. It was my father-in-law who surveyed everything and took a decision. His family honour and reputation were at stake and there he could not take a risk. The man who had never spoken up for me, called me the next morning and said that he did not think it would be safe for me to live in that house. He arranged for my admission to a college, having noticed my interest in reading.

I stayed in the hostel, completed my graduation and then my Masters and went on to become a lecturer. The terrible molestation experience turned out to be the turning point in my life for better days.

So life has very strange ways of unfolding. My job gave me physical, psychological and financial independence and after retirement I chose to come here because as a child we would come here for holidays since an aunt of mine stayed here. I had happy memories. I bought clothes I liked to wear, ate the food I wanted to, even joined dance classes. I chose not to get married though I did have a couple of relationships. My little sensitive niece is like a daughter to me and visits me regularly with her family. I also visit her. She has two children. My family is complete. I kept my lips sealed about what my brother-in-law had done. Life is not white and black. After all it is his daughter who had been my ally in that house."

Dida broke out of her reverie and addressed Romadi. "It is said that it is always darkest before dawn.. You have lived a life of remorse for years. How about changing the setting now? Do you watch the same channel on television all the time?"

Romadi sat up. Pulling herself up from the quicksand of guilt, with a resolute tone she said, "I will find that *tantric* and ask him about the family of that little girl."

"Hmm. And how will that help you?" asked Dida.

Sighing thoughtfully she replied, "I had given him the money and he told me that the deed had been done. Sometimes I wonder about that."

"So you feel that he may have just played on your emotions, taken the money and kept it for himself. And then, finding you vulnerable used you sexually?"

"It...it is possible, isn't it?" she replied, hope underlying her words. "I was emotionally so weak then that I was ready to believe anything that he said. I think I was under a hypnotic spell. It cannot justify the heinous act that I agreed to. Killing a child cannot get you a child. It is the worst kind of superstition I played into."

"So you are not that upset about your husband's mistress or that he will give the son all the property. What you cannot live with is the guilt and remorse of being responsible for a child's murder."

"Yes, absolutely. I heard my neighbour mention the tantric's name the other day. He needs to be exposed. This has to stop. He cannot do this to another."

"But it will also mean exposing yourself. He might threaten to tell people that you slept with him. Are you ready for that?"

Romadi hesitated for a moment and said firmly, her remorse giving her the strength, "Yes, I am. That will be the atonement for my sins. And other young vulnerable women will be saved."

Gramdida met the District Magistrate for the briefing of the events without mentioning the name of the woman involved. In time the man was called in for questioning. Basically a weakling, he gave in easily to the arduous interrogation. He had never killed a child though that was the tactic he used to trap the women. Gauging the money power of his 'client' and the intensity of despair and distress, he would quote an amount, swearing them to complete secrecy if they wanted their wish fulfilled.

He was charged with fraud and cheating.

Romadi embraced Gramdida, tears of relief streaming down.

But what she had not mentioned to Dida or to anyone else was that she was living with the reminder of her 'sins' every single day—knowing that she had nurtured the seeds of the *tantric* in her womb for nine months.

She knew that the other woman's son could not have been sired by her husband.

Life certainly had its way of showing who was in control.

About the Author

Sumita Banerjea is an author and educator. An alumna of the Convent of Jesus and Mary, and St. Stephen's College, New Delhi, she has done her PhD in History on 'Crime Against Women And By Women In Bengal In The 18th And 19th Centuries'. She has written school textbooks on Geography and English and has also written for various newspapers and magazines. During her time as an educator, she conceptualised and edited an anthology of writings by school children in the senior classes. She is also trained in psychological counselling and conducts workshops for corporates, teachers and students.

Her first book of fiction, *Chowringhee Charms* (Readomania 2021) received wonderful reviews.

Sumita loves to experience life in a myriad different ways: travelling, teaching, writing, counselling, listening to happenings in the lives of people from various walks of life, and telling stories. She lives in Kolkata.

Redo

Readomania

Readomania exists to nurture, curate, and bring to you content you love. We are a publishing house that takes pride in encouraging talent, new or old, and provides a wonderful platform for awesome stories.

We make this possible in multiple ways.

The first as an independent publishing house. Readomania boasts of multiple imprints across various categories—fiction, nonfiction, children, to name a few. An eclectic mix of content for its readers, when you read a Readomania title, you enter a world that's yours, supported by unique and quality narratives.

The second, as an online publishing platform for writers—a place to share stories, poems, opinions, travelogues, a way to explore your creative talent. Available as premium, as well as free-to-read content across multiple genres, the reader is spoilt for choice.

Join us in this journey, as we explore, develop, and present stories to our readers and audiences. Welcome to the world of Readomania, get ready to craft stories that enrich lives.

You can visit us at: www.readomania.com